The Door Was Pushed Wider . . .

Sis saw a stack of cartons in the room, and a syringe, bottles, and glass vials on the floor.

Bud gaped at her from the threshold. Then he reached for the doorknob.

"Don't close it!" Sis cried. The thought of being alone with him in the dark aisle terrified her. She'd seen what surely must be drug supplies, and he knew she'd seen them.

Bud spoke in a tone of plain misery. "What—what're you gonna do?"

Sis asked herself the same question. There was only one answer. "I'll have to tell . . ."

DOUBLE STANDARDS

PATSEY GRAY

ACE TEMPO BOOKS, NEW YORK

*To Gerald H. Gray, M.D., my husband,
always young in heart*

DOUBLE STANDARDS

ONE

"GET UP," Sis told herself. But she didn't move. It was great to be away from home, from her father. Now she'd forget to be angry with him, so she'd no longer feel guilt. I'll be a new person in this summer job, she thought. Nobody out here knows why I left home, and nobody has to know.

She lay listening to morning sounds not too different from those of Brown's Mill, Kansas: birds, millions of birds; a horse nickering; the creek's voice down below her apartment. Apartment? Her uncle in his letter had called it that, but it turned out to be a one-room cabin atop a small rise.

On her squeaky cot, Sis inhaled the aroma of Tanbark Ranch, California, in June. It seemed to be a mixture of dry hills and earth mold. She tasted faintly the tang of bay from the huge tree that she'd glimpsed hugging her cabin. Some of its leaves, she now saw,

1

had tumbled in through the window. What she wanted to smell and taste was breakfast, but for that she'd have to wait until the Chuck Wagon opened—so her uncle had told her the previous night.

He'd said, when he met her at the airport, ''You're pretty young to be on your own. Sixteen, if I remember right?'' He remembered wrong, but she didn't correct him. She was nearly sixteen, which she'd tell him as soon as she was settled. In any case she was strong, though she'd never be tall.

During the hour's ride in the pickup, she'd sneaked glances at this uncle whom she hadn't seen in years. Funny that he and her dad, brothers, should have such different careers as horseman and realtor.

Now, this morning, she took the three steps from bed to the only window. She was looking into the upper branches of the bay tree. Its trunk seemed to be all that kept her shack from sliding into the creek.

She crossed the room—another few steps—and opened the door. That must be a covered ring, maybe a city block away. The rocky road to it ran between barns and corrals on one side and, on the other, an oak-studded hill where horses grazed. All around, more distant hills made the area a valley.

In her bathrobe she ran down to ''her'' bathroom, which had a sign, ''Ladies,'' over its door. Some privacy! But who cared? There, facing the mirror, she thought again, brown hair and eyes, how ordinary— and the eyes round at that. But her figure was good, though not yet sexy, and her face had the few freckles it needed, according to her sister Marion.

"It's that bad?" Sis had asked.

"A disaster," Eve kidded.

The three sisters were good friends. Just the same it was a relief to get away from so much talent—Eve, college on a scholarship; Marion, a successful artist already. Those two sometimes shared their stepmother's social life, which held no appeal for Sis.

Shortly, in jeans, sneakers, and T-shirt, she walked into the Chuck Wagon.

"You must be the new kid," the girl behind the counter said.

"Yes, I'm Sis Reynolds."

"I'm Laurie. Coffee?"

"Please." It might sound dumb to ask for milk. "And a doughnut. Maybe two doughnuts."

While Laurie served her, Sis looked around at the western decorations: branding irons, spurs, bits, ropes. Facing Laurie again, she wondered how such a curvy form could have been squeezed into such tight pants and blouse. She herself used no makeup as a rule, only sometimes eye stuff. Almost with envy she gazed at Laurie's cascading black curls and orange lipstick and asked, "Is this where you live?"

"Yeah, me and my husband Ernie," Laurie answered, "at the rear of this building. Lee's office is there, too." Laurie went on, "By the way, if you're staying in that cabin, better hang a curtain at the window."

"But I love seeing out into the tree," Sis told her.

"You see out, somebody else sees in."

Sis laughed. "Who, birds?"

The doors swung in, pushed by her uncle. They were half doors, like those in western bars on TV. His eyes swept the room and evidently found nothing wrong. After a glance at his watch he asked Sis, "Are you settled in? Everything okay?"

She said yes, and he continued, "When you've eaten, then, I'll put you to work. We won't be as rushed as tomorrow, Saturday. But next week, when school's out, every day will be rushed. Which is good, businesswise."

Sis bolted her breakfast and ran out. Bright sunshine and the start of activity all around made her exclaim, "Oh, Uncle Lee, this place and I, it's love at first sight!" With outflung arms she twirled around, then hoped she hadn't seemed childish.

Striding along, her uncle spoke drily. "Let's hope this love affair lasts. But call me Lee. Everyone does."

She trotted to keep up while he led her through the two barns. Both had a feed and a tack room, a blackboard for the day's schedule, and tie and box stalls on each side of an aisle.

In the first barn a young Mexican boy was cleaning stalls, singing a nostalgic-sounding song. An older teenager worked in the second barn, straw in his straw-colored hair and wild patches on his jeans. He must have had an artistic girlfriend.

Past their hearing, Lee said, "Manuel and Bud will

4

stop and lean on their pitchforks if anyone offers to talk. So keep away from 'em. Also, keep your beachwear away, shorts and such. Understand?''

"Yes."

"Likewise no horseplay. The boys get alternate Mondays off,'' Lee continued, walking on toward the ring on its slight elevation. "Those days you'll help muck out and clean the horses' automatic drinking bowls and so on. Other days, you'll teach, groom, and clean tack. The older clients—we have Grandma Day once a month—you have to nursemaid those. See they don't strangle a horse tying it, or turn it loose.'' He gave a snort that wasn't humorous. "You'll hear 'em: 'Oh, Lee, my saddle's coming off!' 'Lee, is this Stormy or is it Bandit?' ''

Sis laughed. She would have laughed at just about anything this morning. The horses' names tickled her. She supposed they'd been chosen to make the rider, child or grandma, think she was mastering a wild one. She didn't care that Lee hadn't mentioned any day off for her.

He paused to wave at some youngsters arriving in a station wagon. To the driver he shouted, "With you in a minute.'' While the kids dashed to the Chuck Wagon, he spoke again to Sis about her work. Listening, she gazed around with pleasure, breathed in odors of feed and manure, and watched a couple of chickens scratch for grain. The smell of hay bales stacked behind the barns reached her, too.

"I'm not paying you much," Lee said, "being you're still green. You never owned a horse, did you?"

Sis said no, without adding that she'd always wanted one. "Most days I exercised horses at the riding school," she explained, "and I learned to jump. A show rider coached me, in trade for my care of his mare. Lots of times he had me jump her in shows. And I do own the English saddle I brought."

Lee nodded. "That's the point, as I told your dad. Not many here ride English, but I need help with those who do."

How great if she could get in some jumping, Sis thought; better yet, show jumping. But on what?

Another car's approach hurried Lee's next words. "Let's go saddle for the beginners' lesson in the ring. They're the under-tens, and I'm not used to teaching that age. The girl before you did that. You like kids?"

"Yes, I really do," Sis answered.

In the first barn, Manuel's barn, she followed Lee's example: brought tack from the tackroom, saddled and bridled the rent horses in their tie stalls, then backed them out for the children. The kids loved their homely old mounts, and patted legs or stomachs, and kissed noses.

Only one little girl reproved Sis. "You didn't make us brush."

"Your teeth?"

Giggles. "*No*! We're s'posed to brush our horses, and their manes if we can reach. You do their tails in case they kick."

"Lucky me," said Sis.

"What's your name?" a small redhead asked her.
"Sis."

"*Miss* Sis? That sounds like Ms." More giggles.

In turn Sis asked, "Who helped you guys before I showed up?"

"Oh, a lady," she was told. "She left after Blackie bit her."

"I see. Which one is Blackie?"

"The black one, of course." Giggle. "Over there. But it wasn't his fault. She punched his stomach with her knee because he swells when you cinch him. You want to meet Lee's cat? His name is Burper, and he really, really burps."

Up in the ring, Lee stood in the center, repeating orders, each one a dozen times. "Don't slump." "Loosen your reins." "Heels down." So on and on.

These children were too young to do more than walk, jog, and briefly lope. Their horses, wise to them, constantly stopped at the ring gate or in the center, from which Lee chased them. The littlest boy fell from an almost motionless pony, then bragged, "Fury bucked me off!" Fury was a toy Shetland, obviously a general pet. Another child ran from the ring toward the rest room, leaving a loose horse.

Sis caught the horse and led it to Lee, who said, "I've about had it. Take over, will you, but go easy. And if the parents give you trouble, send them to me," and he indicated drivers in the cars parked at the Chuck Wagon.

Soon Sis was telling her pupils, "We'll spend the last five minutes on a game. What'll it be?"

"Tag, Ms.," the redhead cried. And when a redheaded mother came up after the class, Sis was introduced as "Ms., who's a neat teacher."

"I'll handle the next lesson," Lee told Sis. "It's a private. You can be getting these horses ready for the intermediates. Water 'em and loosen cinches, but don't forget to cinch up again. And while you're resting, put some salve on Dynamite's withers. The boys'll show you."

Sis liked the intermediates less than the beginners. They were inclined to eye her warily, to whisper and make jokes. Also, the ring was poorly ventilated so that a film of tanbark dust hung in the air. Light and air entered only through a two- to three-foot opening that circled the top of the walls except where posts supported the roof. She was glad when it was time to get outdoors again. Better yet, Lee said that after lunch she might take a client for an hour's trail ride.

"All you'll have to do is follow Mrs. Ashby," he said. "She'll ride her own mare. For yourself, check the blackboard, and use any one of the rent horses that hasn't been out."

Once more, at noon, Sis felt the satisfaction of opening the door of her own house. If I really owned it, she thought, I'd make it cute. But it needed a few things, mainly a lamp. The bare bulb hanging down was horrible, especially for one who loved to read in bed.

Without a chair, she sat on the cot to eat her snack and listen to the voice of the creek. She imagined the water smelled fresh and reedy, having seen it bouncing over a rocky bed between cool dark banks of ferns. While she daydreamed, a gray squirrel appeared at the open window. At sight of her, he lashed his tail, chattered something indignant, and whisked away.

She wondered about her uncle. He seemed a hard worker, gruff, with little humor. As she pictured him, she heard him call her, and went to open the door.

He was in his pickup. Leaning out, he offered, "I'll trust you with this pickup tomorrow if you need anything from the store. It's only a couple of miles, at a small place called the Junction, where I live. The restaurant's there too, Blanche's."

Sis backed a step into the room.

"Okay?" Lee called.

"I don't—don't have my driver's license," she blurted.

He looked annoyed, saying, "If you're that forgetful, you and I may not get along. Write home for it tonight." He was gunning his motor.

"But—" She hesitated, seeing he'd misunderstood.

"What? I'm in a hurry."

Panicked, she couldn't find words, and he drove off, spurting dust.

Sis shut the door and wandered back to her cot. "Idiot," she called herself. "Why did you let him think you were sixteen, with a driver's license?''

As usual in troubled moments, one hand went to her lips, and she nibbled her nails. Then she thought, so I'm like my father after all. Dad had sold a lot for a client, then he'd bought the lot himself from the buyer and resold it at a higher price. He'd made more money for himself than for his client.

Sis wondered again if her stepmother, Mimi, knew that. Marion and Eve knew, but it didn't seem to bother them. They claimed such deals were common, and that Sis's standards were unrealistic. Yet right off she'd been dishonest with Lee. What a dummy!

Well, it wasn't the end of the world. Sis shook herself. She was making a big thing out of nothing.

"Cool it," she said. "And this afternoon, level with Lee."

TWO

AT TWO O'CLOCK that afternoon, Sis found both boys in the second barn. Bud, the bigger one, told her Lee had gone to buy feed and wouldn't be back for at least an hour.

She said with a twinge of panic, "I'm supposed to take Mrs. Ashby out."

"Her mare's ready. That's Twinkle." He pointed to a lightweight chestnut looking from her box stall. Then he went on, "Lee said for you to ride Gull instead of a rent horse."

"Gull?"

"Lee's gelding, Seagull." Bud snickered. "He's kind of a nut. Mostly we just lunge him. He needs more work, and Lee don't have the time, though I gotta say he has the guts."

"Why would he need guts?" Sis asked.

"Gull's mean," Bud answered.

Sis guessed that he, and possibly Lee, wanted to test her. So she said merely, "If you'll show me Gull and his bridle, I'll get my saddle. He'll go English, won't he?"

"Will he! Eh, Manuel?" Bud asked his partner with a grin.

The boys seemed to understand each other, though apparently Manuel didn't speak much English. Now he answered with motions that Bud translated as, "Gull's a jumper."

Within minutes Sis was back, saddling a thin gray thoroughbred in his box stall. He must measure close to seventeen hands, she judged, with a deep girth, broad chest, and well-bred head. He was really built. But his eyes and ears were watchful, and his nostrils flared in and out, questioning the scent of a stranger. He ducked from her hand raised to adjust his bridle, and jumped when one of the boys shouted.

As she led him from the stall, she noticed the door next to it marked "Storeroom." Evidently it was a room between two stalls, a private room, padlocked.

Feeling Gull shy behind her, she wondered how and when he'd been abused. No doubt he had reason to be mean; he wasn't born that way. But he showed no signs of meanness now, and surely Lee wouldn't give her a vicious horse to handle.

If she could have just a little while alone with Gull to gain his confidence . . . only, of course, it would take longer than that. But why not, if Lee agreed? She'd gentled other freaky horses. It'd be almost as if she owned him!

A few minutes later, Bud stood watching the riders leave, probably still hopeful of trouble.

"Vulture," Sis muttered.

His watching wasn't lost on Mrs. Ashby, who remarked, "When Lee's gone, Bud and Manuel slack off. But I suppose most teenagers would. I have one myself. Or maybe Bud's surprised that you should be riding Gull."

Mrs. Ashby appeared to be in her forties. She had on a tailored blue shirt, frontier pants, and polished boots, and a scarf over her hair. It seemed odd that she should hire an escort for a mild trail ride. She couldn't expect problems from her mare Twinkle, who ambled amiably on a loose rein. Rides like this, plus the board of her mare, must cost her plenty. But maybe she wasn't strong.

The horses started out between the barns. After passing the boys' house trailer and the stacked hay, they crossed the creek on a wooden bridge where Gull danced a little. No wonder, for his shoes rang on the boards, and cracks between these showed rushing water below. Beyond the bridge, markers pointed to different trails.

Once on Redwood Trail he grew calmer behind Twinkle. They paralleled the creek into deepening woods where light dimmed and the only sound was the water's. Redwood needles muffled their steps and scented the air.

"Lovely, isn't it?" Mrs. Ashby said over her shoulder.

Sis agreed. It was always lovely to be on horseback. Besides that, she was glad that on the flight west she'd studied about the birds and flowers of California.

They'd been out less than fifteen minutes when Mrs. Ashby called back, "We'll stop and rest around the next bend."

Rest? Sis had been counting on exercise to relax Gull.

Soon Mrs. Ashby turned from the trail to push through a stand of trees. Next to a large willow she dismounted, saying, "I sometimes take a little breather here."

Sis, too, dismounted, though she didn't know why.

Mrs. Ashby said vaguely, "I'll just sit under my favorite tree here." Speaking, she parted the willow fronds and disappeared.

Sis stared at the swinging fronds. What was she supposed to do?

When Gull had grown too impatient, she cleared her throat and asked, "Are you all right, Mrs. Ashby?"

"Fine," the answer floated out.

Silence again. Sis was perspiring. She wished somebody would come along. Then she hoped no one would, for she wouldn't know what to say. With reins in both hands, she couldn't even mop her face. Gull was pawing, churning redwood dust and needles. She asked, more loudly than she intended, "Shouldn't we be leaving?"

At that Mrs. Ashby stepped out. She seemed all right—thank goodness, Sis thought, and said, "I guess we ought to hurry. Lee said an hour."

Mrs. Ashby smiled, and took her reins. "Oh, Lee won't mind if we're a little late. No one else will be waiting for either Twinkle or Gull." Mounted, she urged her mare forward and went on, "By the way, you needn't mention my little detour. It's just my form of relaxation."

Sis watched Mrs. Ashby ahead with half her attention, the other half being on Gull. At the jog now, he wasn't giving her any trouble. She stroked his dusty neck, and decided to ask if she might give him a bath. There were lots of nice little things she could do to make Gull happier—to make her happier, too, if she could pop him over a jump now and then.

A bit later Mrs. Ashby said, "You must come and visit us. We'd love to have you to dinner some evening. I don't see enough friends since—"

Since what, Sis wondered. Startled, she thanked Mrs. Ashby. She wasn't turning down a free home-cooked meal. Besides, she was curious about Mrs. Ashby, and who the "we" included. Not to lose the chance, she called, "How would I get to your home?"

"It's in Berkeley. We'll pick you up. Say tomorrow, about six?"

"I'll be ready." She'd have to wear either her peasant dress, Sis reflected, or her green slacks with the flowered blouse.

She guessed they had passed the halfway mark when Twinkle picked up speed. Both horses broke into a lope, giving her visions of their bolting for home. From the way Gull pulled, this should suit him fine. They'd skid to a stop there, lathered; she'd be fired; and Mrs. Ashby would have fallen off and busted her silly head.

With relief she heard Mrs. Ashby say, "We musn't bring the horses in hot."

Back at the stables, Lee had paused behind a group of youngsters starting toward the ring. He frowned at Sis, saying, "You're late. I was delayed at the feed store, so there was no one to supervise these kids. Now their hour's half over. The parents won't hold still for paying full time."

Sis mumbled an apology, not wanting to tell on Mrs. Ashby. Then she said, "Thank you for letting me ride Gull. Is it true he jumps?"

"He did jump," Lee answered, "till he was knocked around so much he turned nervous and at times nasty. But right now, take this class. I have to store the feed."

Lee went off somewhat appeased, Sis guessed by his walk. Funny how a person's walk showed his mood. She stopped to consider this. Manuel moved slowly, sadly: homesick. Bud swaggered: cocky. And look, Burper, the orange cat, stalking a bird: sly. And she, Sis, had better *run* to her class. A wail had come from the ring, "This horse hates me!"

Again her students were beginners, cute, eager kids. She felt rewarded when the one whose horse "hated" her announced that the horse liked her now since she'd learned to ride.

When she led her group back to the barn, Lee was still stacking hay. He sent her to the ring again for the final class of the day. Now the tanbark dust was really getting to her. She tasted it, felt it on her skin, and saw it floating in the shafts of light that slanted down.

Discomfort made her grumpy. She had told her students temporarily to ride without stirrups, in order to judge if they sat the jog smoothly. But a fat girl named Patty kept slipping her feet into the stirrups whenever she thought herself out of sight.

"Patty, you're not fooling me," Sis told her. "I know when your feet are in the stirrups."

Patty ignored that, looking sullen.

"That's cheating," Sis snapped.

"So what? Everybody cheats."

"They do at school," a voice said.

"Billy did, at our swim meet," another put in.

Standing there, Sis was struck by the same depression she'd known at home. Here it was again, the cheating, in school and sports, as the kids said, and, from what she heard, in business and politics as well. If you didn't cheat, you were "different," or stupid. You should think nothing of a real estate deal where the seller lost money unfairly.

Sis realized suddenly that the children had stopped

their horses. She made an effort. "In *my* class, nobody cheats. Okay, let's try it again. Patty, you can stay if you'll play fair. Otherwise, get lost."

She was still too angry to wonder if the kids would take this, or to care that Patty left the ring, no doubt to complain to Lee.

After the class, Lee called her and asked about the Patty incident. Patty had given him her version; now Sis gave hers.

"You mustn't be too rough on the kids," Lee said. "They quit, we're out of business. But Patty won't last long anyway. She's only riding to lose weight."

They were standing in the parking lot, while the remaining children charged through the swinging doors of the Wagon, as they called it. Sis whipped up her nerve to say, "Uncle—er, Lee, there's something I have to tell you."

"Oh?" He looked almost amused. "Who else have you bawled out?"

"It's about my age," she blurted. "I'm fifteen, not sixteen. Not quite sixteen."

He frowned, but then he said, "Well, you're here, so what's the difference." That was all.

Sis blew a sigh of relief. Now she could enjoy the late afternoon, which shadowed the base of the surrounding hills, leaving their summits in sunlight. Sounds of munching came from the barns, where the boys had fed. Occasionally, some horse rattled a pan or bucket. Across the fence, hay had been forked to those in pasture, who shouldered one another from the piles with squeals and nips.

Her work finished, Sis decided to buy her supper before Laurie locked up. She felt good that Lee wasn't upset either about her age or about Patty. Marion and Eve were right, she decided. She was too darn critical even of herself. Fifteen, sixteen, big deal!

The half hour Sis spent with Laurie convinced her that Laurie could be fun, although older—maybe twenty-two or three.

"I was married once before," Laurie informed her. "Ernie works nights, pumping gas at the all-night station on the freeway."

After a while Sis asked, "How well do you know Mrs. Ashby?"

Laurie lit a cigarette and answered through a cloud of smoke. "Seems she went to pieces when her husband died five months ago. It was hard on both her and her son Jeff."

Oh, a son, thought Sis. Somehow she had pictured Mrs. Ashby's teenager as a girl. . . .

Sis finished her pizza and asked for pie.

"But," Sis continued, "wouldn't Lee mind that she rests while on rides?"

"Why should he? If he complained, he might lose her as a client, and all that man cares about is business. Oh, he's okay to work for as long as you adore work and do it right—his way."

Sis approved of that. She admired a perfectionist.

"*And*," Laurie went on, "you gotta work super hard to prove you're as good as a boy, which Lee doesn't admit. But one thing folks say for him, he's good to his horses. I guess that's because they're his livelihood."

Sis watched Laurie puff her cigarette.

As she reached her cabin, she said aloud, "My home." Then, to the squirrel at the window, "Our home." She hoped it was the same squirrel as yesterday's. A pet, at last, difficult in town. This one had a crooked ear, by which she'd recognize him. Behind him, foliage had darkened, and on all sides little wild neighbors twittered and rustled, about to retire.

"Cozy," she said, sinking onto her cot. Tonight she'd read for hours. She'd have to buy herself a lamp and more magazines. Maybe the Ashbys would advise her about shopping.

She pictured Mrs. Ashby. Poor thing, trying to bury her grief over her husband's death.

She wandered to her open door to gaze out absently. The boys' trailer wasn't visible from here, but Laurie's lights looked friendly. Uneasily, she realized that, though no longer deceiving Lee about her age, she wondered if she'd have to keep it up before Jeff, and began to wish she weren't going to their home. If only she were sophisticated, she'd know how to act. Two lines of poetry, read somewhere, jumped to her mind:

DOUBLE STANDARDS

*"Oh, what a tangled web we weave
When first we practice to deceive."*

THREE

HAVING READ LATE, Sis slept next morning until her alarm woke her with a hideous clatter in the cool green room. She heard no human noises outside, but the air was alive with bird talk and horse talk.

Blinking, she stepped into the lightening day in robe and pajamas, clutching towel and toilet kit. After a self-conscious glance around, she raced down to the rest room and darted in.

Out again, showered, dressed, and combed, and up to the cabin once more. Before going in, she paused to admire a sight straight from a western picture. A rider was driving the horses down off the crest of the pasture hill toward the barns. She could make out it was Lee, his face shaded by his western straw hat, long legs in jeans hanging comfortably, his spurs glinting in the early-sunlight. He was bareback. Now and then his right hand slapped his thigh while he hollered at some balky horse. It wasn't Gull he rode; probably one of the rent horses. How cleverly these cow ponies hopped and slithered down the steep slope on the slick dry grass! Lee began to whistle, as if he were enjoying himself.

"Almost human," Sis said, and ducked into her room. It warmed her to recall Laurie's words, "He's good to his horses." Making the bed, she caught sight of her fingernails. They looked quite decent, not freshly gnawed. That was lucky, since she'd meet new people tonight. She'd have to wash her hair before going. Newly washed, it had a nice shine.

Maybe Jeff would fall for her. She would try to fall for him, just because it was time she had a regular boy friend. The fact that she didn't have one hadn't mattered so far, because her crowd moved in groups, not twosomes. Oh, one boy had fallen for her, so suddenly he'd about scared her to death. She thought now there should be a way to skip the years between being a crude kid and an adult. Maybe some new clothes would help her look mature.

"When is payday?" she asked Laurie at breakfast.

"First and fifteenth," said Laurie, smacking down a glass of milk on the counter. "But if you're short, say so. I'll loan you something."

"Thanks, but I can make it," Sis answered. She still had money from home, and no expenses except meals.

They'd been ignoring Bud, who'd come in to buy a doughnut and now stood listening. He said to Sis with a smirk, ''I'll stake you, sweetheart.''

''Scram, microbe,'' Laurie ordered him.

Bud sauntered out, just as Lee was heard to roar something about worthless barn boys.

''You don't like Bud?'' Sis asked Laurie.

''That type, you gotta step on,'' Laurie answered. And she added darkly. ''He's smarter than he looks. Older, too. He got the best of me twice with his bets.''

''Bets on horses?''

''What else? That's all he knows, except he's a fair mechanic. That's why Lee keeps him. He's handy with the van and pickup, and when the mothers have car trouble. But before a horse show, see, he'll bet you on one of our horses to place or win.'' Sis wasn't interested in betting, but she thought that some day it would be fun to outsmart Bud.

This being Saturday, kids were arriving every few minutes, coming from homes and farms near the ranch. Tnose who couldn't afford to rent a horse or take a lesson came anyway to watch or just be near a horse, any horse. They came on foot or on bicycles, and even the smallest asked for work, claiming to be older than they looked. Sis sympathized. She'd done the same at their age. Others, the brats, were left by mothers who then sped away.

''Those women take me for a blasted baby-sitter,'' Lee complained. ''Last week one of their kids started a fire in the phone booth—right alongside the Wagon and my office!''

"It's lucky they can't get into your storeroom," Sis remarked.

"That's why it's locked," Lee said. "What's there is junk, except my gun. That's just for an emergency. I'd lock the office too, only I'm in and out all day."

At noon he asked her, "You want to eat or ride?"

"Ride." She'd been starving, but instantly forgot it.

"Then get your boots on," he ordered, "and saddle Gull. I'll set up a few jumps in the ring, and you show me how you handle him."

Breathless, Sis ran to her cabin. Her fingers fumbled while she changed sneakers for boots. Jumping was a thrill, but it had been weeks since she'd jumped. She felt in her stomach the start of that lovely, almost sick sensation, mixed fear and elation, dread and eagerness.

I'm ridiculous, she thought. Why do I get in such a stew every time? But the sick feeling would last only until she was on her horse. Once on, she'd always been okay, except a couple of times when she was younger. She'd actually been sick, and just about died of shame.

As soon as she joined Gull, she saw that he knew her intention. Maybe her manner told him, or the English saddle did. When he'd stepped from his box stall, he flung up his head to face toward the ring. He snorted, and his eyes warned, don't force me to do what I hate.

"It's all right, old boy," she said, leading him outside. "Don't worry, we'll have fun. See, no whip, no spurs, and a nice, easy snaffle bit. So stand still a minute, will you, while I get on."

She didn't want an audience at her first attempt to jump Gull. But in the ring she found not only Lee but the two boys. For a good laugh, she thought, or to help pick me up. No, they'd probably let me lie there. Lee hadn't much in the way of jumps, since most people here rode western. So the boys set up only a post and rails at one side of the ring, and a brush jump at the other. Sis guessed the height of each might be about three foot six. From her elevation on Gull, they didn't look alarming.

They shouldn't have alarmed him either, but when he'd pussyfooted into the ring, he eyed them as if they were alive and might attack him.

"Just walk him around a few minutes," Lee directed. "Relax, and maybe he will."

But Gull stepped stiff-legged and breathed in loud snorts. He tried to avoid going close to either jump. After only a short time, the veins in his neck stood out where sweat dampened it. He chomped his bit so violently that flecks of foam flew back as if he were really a gull, skimming a wave.

From the center where the boys watched, Bud said happily, "He's sure excited."

Excited! Explosive was more like it, Sis thought. It seemed a contradiction to work hard at relaxing a horse, but she'd nearly always been able to do so.

She hummed a soothing tune, and nodded agreement

when Lee said, "Okay, trot now. Trot figure eights, change directions, all like that till he settles down."

"That might be tomorrow," Bud chuckled, and Lee snapped at him, "Shut up."

Without raising her voice Sis asked, as she passed them, "What's scared him so?"

"Bad handling." Lee's voice followed her. "Last year a guy leased him and just about wrecked him. That ended with one heck of a crash at a stone wall. We ought to build one, so he can get over fearing it. Then the girl before you here wasn't gutsy enough to do anything with him. And I don't ride English myself. I only got him on a trade for a worse horse."

When Gull was breathing easier, Sis looked over at Lee and said, "Canter?"

He nodded, and she tightened her legs. Gull responded with a bound, and more bounds that gradually subsided into an erratic lope. With faked nonchalance she reversed.

After many minutes of this, Gull dropped his head a little, evened his stride, and seemed at last to be settling down somewhat. Seeing this, Lee said, low, "Whenever you're ready."

Sis took a deeper seat and with sneaky fingers shortened her reins. Suddenly and smoothly, she faced Gull into the brush jump. Taken by surprise, he jumped it as if it were five feet high. Sis, too, was surprised, nearly unseated, by the power of his leap.

"Now the post and rails," Lee said.

But this time Gull was wary and became, as before, a bomb ready to explode. Sis knew she ought to follow orders. But instead she followed her own instinct. She circled past the jumps and around the ring until Gull had relaxed. Then she sent him at the post and rails, which he cleared with space to spare. Landing, she heard Lee say, "That's all." He sounded thoughtful.

But how disappointing to quit now! "What a terrific horse!" Sis exclaimed. "I bet he could win jumper classes anywhere."

"He has," Lee answered. "But at a show usually he gets too nervous to know what he's doing. Even here, though he understands we're just schooling, you see how he works himself up."

"I'd like to try building his confidence, little by little," Sis ventured.

While Manuel walked Gull to cool him and Bud cleared away the jumps, Lee reasoned against Sis's idea.

"During your 'little by little,' " he said, "I'm paying the boys to feed and clean Gull, *and* buying his feed. I ought to sell him."

"I'll clean and feed him," Sis said quickly, "and do his stall. I'd like to. You'd only have to buy the feed." And, she added silently, that way I could fatten him up.

For several minutes, Lee appeared to be calculating, not exactly thrilled. Finally, he said, "All right, you feed and clean, I'll buy. But don't expect extra pay. This is your choice. As far as quieting Gull, you'd be doing it the hard way—which would be my way, too. Oh, I know some shortcuts that'd serve, but I won't use 'em. Maybe I'm a fool.''

Sis waited, inhaling tanbark dust, hearing Gull's muffled hoofsteps on it, thinking about shortcuts. She'd seen them used at the riding school—cruel methods, gimmicks, force. Lee must have a heart, she decided, for in spite of what Laurie said, he was giving Gull a break even though Gull earned nothing. She persevered, ''You'll let me handle him, then?''

''Go ahead, for a couple of weeks. Mind, I'm only willing because you showed me what I hoped to see, that you have a little savvy. But Gull showed me he hasn't changed, and I doubt he ever will.''

To help her cause, Sis said, ''Where I rode in Brown's Mill, they claimed I do pretty well with problem horses. So if it's okay, I'll ride Gull every day, not schooling much, just pleasure rides.''

''*Pleasure*?'' Lee grinned. ''Help yourself. You can show me results at the next horse show. But if you get hurt, home you go. Which reminds me, don't you have a hunt cap?''

''Yes, but it's so hot, I thought—''

''Next time, wear it,'' Lee ordered.

During the busy afternoon, Sis's thoughts were on Gull. She learned from the children that they competed at horse shows throughout the summer. The next one would be at the end of the month, a schooling show at Windy Hill. Melissa Murphy, her favorite of the under-tens, confided, "I never win anything. Usually I fall off."

"But you still like to go?"

"Oh, yes, Ms. 'Specially the overnight times, at the fairs, where there's a roller coaster, and lots of scream-ing and loud stuff. At one fair, they shoot this lady out of a cannon, bang!" Melissa bounced her red curls in glee.

Screams, bangs, and cannons—just what Gull needed!

By late afternoon, Sis was thinking of the evening ahead at the Ashbys'. When at last she was free, she hurried to shower and to shampoo her cap of short hair.

After she'd put on her green slacks and the blouse, she added the little gold heart-shaped earrings that her sisters said matched the glints in her eyes. She said good-bye to the squirrel at the window, and "I'll try to bring you a squirrel bag tonight." Lastly, she set her alarm for extra early next morning. She would have to feed Gull and clean his stall when the boys fed and cleaned, or he'd start an uproar.

A car braked outside, and she snatched her white sweater and stepped out.

A boy—older, she thought—smiled at her from his Volkswagen and called up, "I'm Jeff Ashby." As she joined him, she saw surprise in his blue eyes when he went on, "Maybe you aren't Sis. I was expecting a grim sort of Amazon type."

"I'm sorry," she said primly, "if your mother got

that impression."

"Oh, not at all. Mother didn't—she just—"

"Got that impression." Sis laughed, smug at sounding so composed.

Jeff talked easily while they wound out the ranch road, past the crossroads marked Junction, where Blanche's Place was already lit up. He had a throaty chuckle that was cute, as if he were privately laughing at her, but also kind of pleased with her. Of course, it didn't matter, since he must be at least seventeen, maybe eighteen. He'd probably die of boredom tonight. Well, this outing hadn't been *her* idea. She was Mrs. Ashby's date, not Jeff's.

She saw by stealthy glances that his hair was a sun-bleached thatch above his tan. His hands on the wheel were tanned, too. He drove with assurance on the freeway nearing Berkeley.

"Going up," he said suddenly, and swung off on a side street. They climbed up steep S turns, past homes perched on what looked like cliffs compared to the flat of Brown's Mill. From decks and balconies, the occupants looked west over the bay, the two great bridges festooned with lights, and San Francisco between them, twinkling on its hills.

At the Ashby home, they walked through to a deck overlooking the view. Mrs. Ashby met them, and before long the three sat down to dinner, still on the deck. It seemed funny, old-fashioned or something, to be eating with just a boy and his mother. Sis's social evenings usually had been haphazard; disorganized, her stepmother called them. It was true her crowd seldom knew where they were going or when.

Refusing help, Mrs. Ashby went to the kitchen and back whenever necessary. She struck Sis as pathetic, for when she sat withdrawn, sadness was there on her face.

In the course of talk, the subject of jobs came up. Jeff was working as a carpenter's helper here in Berkeley, a summer job. Five months ago, he said, when his mother started to ride, he'd worked weekends for Lee.

Sis considered this while sounds of the city drifted up and night sharpened the lights across the bay. She assumed Mrs. Ashby had taken up riding as a distraction after her husband's death. Presently she asked Jeff, "Did you ever know Sea Gull?"

"I sure did."

"So tell me about him."

Mrs. Ashby went to the kitchen, and Jeff spoke of Gull, his ability, his good looks, his nervousness. "About six months ago at a horse show I saw him jump well, like a different horse. I have no idea why, not being a real horseman."

"Lee must have known why," Sis said.

"Lee wasn't there. He was sick, and somebody else hauled the horses to the show. The girl you replaced rode Gull, and she was scared of him, so all the more credit to them both."

"Did you ever see Gull act mean?" Sis asked.

Jeff grinned. "I saw him dump a cowboy who was too free with the spurs. It was probably one of the few times Lee ever laughed. That made the other guy mad, and he said, 'Let's see *you* ride this horse.' The stirrups were too short, but Lee swung on, just casual, and with a loose rein Gull walked off like a gentleman. Lee put him into a lope, and when Gull got a little snorty Lee just told him to knock it off, and he did."

"That's my idea of horsemanship," Sis said.

She described in detail her plans for Gull, then was silent. A burst of laughter rose from some garden below.

Jeff's hair shone in the dim light; his eyes were teasing as he asked, "You're dead serious about reforming Gull, aren't you?"

"Yes, I am." That sounded stuffy.

"Well, good luck." Was he laughing at her, thinking that where others had failed, she was crazy to expect success?

She felt horribly stiff. Staring straight out at the city lights, she refused to look at him, though she knew he was looking at her. She knew it without raising her eyes. Seconds ticked on and on. The silence had a strange, self-conscious quality. But it had lasted too long. Move, she begged herself, say something. But she couldn't. She had turned to wood.

Mrs. Ashby's steps approached, and Sis jumped up to leave. She remembered her squirrel, but she couldn't ask for a squirrel bag—it would be embarrassing.

Before his mother came out, Jeff asked with his chuckle, "Did anyone ever tell you you're different?"

More than once! But this was the first time it had sounded nice.

And then he had to spoil it by reaching to tousle her hair, exactly as if she were one of the under-tens.

FOUR

TWO FRIDAYS LATER, Sis's alarm shrilled earlier than usual.

Right away, she remembered: she was to jump Gull for a friend of Lee's. Why, and what friend, she didn't know. Lee's orders were to meet at six, so they'd have the ring to themselves.

On her feet, she realized the room was stuffy. Even the floorboards were warm. So, open the door. There's nobody around at this hour. No one stirring, not Burper or the chickens, or the rent horses up on the hill. How lovely it was out, in the cool dawn. Yet there was a breathless quality that meant heat later. All week the weather had been building up to a hot spell.

I've been here over two weeks? Not possible, Sis thought, pulling on her jeans. Each day the ranch and people had become more real to her. She was learning that Lee had his good points. You could count on his being always the same. But Laurie's toughness was part act. Sis knew too what Mrs. Ashby needed; that Jeff could be her friend, if not exactly her boy friend. Most important, they'd all accepted her.

Ten minutes later, Gull greeted her with a mumble, which she returned with a hug. She thought of this barn as his, his and Bud's. The other barn was Manuel's. From the feed room she brought him a quarter pan of alfalfa meal, then dropped half a flake of hay in his manger. He'd get the rest of his breakfast after work. He hardly minded lately that she cleaned his stall while he ate, to save time. So now she fetched one of the manure carts and shoveled his droppings into it. His stall was bedded in shavings, although these were more expensive than straw. She always loved to open a fresh bale, to see the clean, blond shavings pour out, smelling of pine or fir. But nobody here opened anything without Lee's okay. "Ol' Lee counts every blade and every grain," Bud said.

Sis emptied the cart at the pile behind the barn, then borrowed a box of grooming tools; some day, she'd buy Gull his own. She didn't approve of brushing a horse while he ate; he should be left alone. But this morning, with time pressing, she had no choice.

As she talked, gradually Gull relaxed. Once he tried to mumble at her with his mouth full, and only managed a gargle that was so comical she laughed out loud. She kept away from his head, so as not to annoy him, and worked on his hindquarters and tail. Brushing hard uncovered faint dark spots that she hoped would be dapples if he were ever clean enough.

When he'd finished eating, she haltered him, led him out, and cross-tied him in the aisle, one rope snapped to a ring in either wall. Worried about time, she glanced at Lee's storeroom, but of course it was locked. She couldn't remember if there was a clock inside, though she'd looked in once when he'd left the door open. It was a dreary place, a barely remodeled stall. A skylight lit it, and dusty old boxes filled it—rubbish, she'd thought, that should be thrown out.

Now, in the aisle, she picked up Gull's feet one by one and cleaned each with the hoof pick. She just couldn't imagine he would ever kick or strike at her. Then she finished brushing, and wet down his mane and foretop, and sponged eyes and nostrils. For a special touch, she borrowed Mrs. Ashby's hoof grease and greased his hoofs.

"There, now you look elegant," she told him, standing back to admire. She would have loved to braid his mane and tail and trim his ears, like a show hunter's. "Ooops, fly spray." And she ran for the plastic container and enveloped them both in mist.

She took a few minutes to shine her saddle and Gull's bridle, and to polish the stirrups and snaffle bit. A look into the tackroom mirror showed her face flushed with heat already, and hair untidy. Darn, no comb. Oh, well.

She wet her hands under a faucet, smacked down her hair, dampened her face and gulped a mouthful of water, breakfast. Now, her hunt cap, and change sneakers for boots. Lee wouldn't allow riding in sneakers, and he'd fire anyone for bare feet. Hear the rooster? Let's go. We'll just have time to warm up. Hey, my stomach's okay.

The ring was cool and dim when Gull catwalked in, snorting a bit under his breath. Sis was surprised to see several jumps, which Lee must have set up last night. She ignored them as she first walked, then trotted Gull all around. Passing the entrance, she caught sight of a gold-colored car by the Chuck Wagon. It looked like a Corvette, and positively glittered in the early sun rays.

Soon at close range she saw that the car's owner, a heavy young man, glittered too, with a diamond ring and gold belt buckle. Ugh. There were no introductions, only Lee's orders, "Show Mr. Kramer what Gull can do. Take several fences, any ones, in both directions." Lee's eyes approved Gull's grooming.

Usually, when Sis had ridden for a few minutes, she could interpret her horse's attitude. This morning the signs told her Gull was going to be good. He'd passed the jumps without shying, he'd quit snorting, he was bridling nicely. Still she didn't hurry him, but cantered steadily on the rail until she saw Lee look at his wristwatch. This, she had learned, meant "Get to work."

She headed for the brush jump, and immediately

Gull tensed. But she sent him on over it, then over a white panel, then the post and rails. He was jumping big and rough, clearing his fences with ease. Sis felt a surge of pride. She changed directions, and Gull slowed, eyeing the brush with mistrust. "Silly," she muttered, and urged him on with legs and voice. He put in a short stride in front of the brush, then jumped it awkwardly, too fast. The next two fences were better although he was hurrying, as if to get the work over. *But he's not freaked out,* Sis thought. She was pleased with him, and told him so.

Lee motioned her to the center, where the men stood. "That'll do," he said.

While she led Gull around to cool him, she tried to overhear the men's talk. The only phrase she caught was Lee's, "You're still interested, Karl?" She watched the two leave, and instantly disliked Karl Kramer when he kicked at Burper. The cat had come to be petted, and burped. What harm was that?

When Sis next saw Lee she was preparing to teach an English rider. She'd been dying to find out what Lee meant by asking if Mr. Kramer was still interested in Gull. Not in *buying* Gull? That would be awful! Maybe in showing him? But Lee didn't like questions from his help, and seldom answered them.

Her silence was rewarded when he said, "I don't believe you're doing Gull any harm." To herself she translated this into "You're doing a fantastic job."

"We'll haul him to the Windy Hill schooling show

next Sunday," Lee went on, "if there's room in the van, and if he continues to improve."

Sis drew in a sharp breath. Skipping Lee's "ifs," she asked faintly, "You mean, enter him in the show?"

"That's the idea," said Lee.

"Who'll show him?"

When he answered "You will," she tried not to look insanely happy. But then Lee spoke again, as if to himself. "I don't *want* to sell the horse. I know he has ability. If I could just put my finger on why he goes so well at some shows . . ."

So he *was* thinking of selling Gull to Mr. Kramer, Sis realized with dismay. If she'd known that, she could have brought out the worst in Gull this morning. Only that would have been cheating. . . .

That day was the first of a hectic week. As the heat increased, it affected different people differently. Lee appeared unmoved as ever, no matter how much he sweated. Laurie wore thinner blouses, and got mad when her mascara ran. Manuel drooped, and so did the rent horses. Bud evaded work whenever he dared.

Sis didn't mind the heat much because it lessened Gull's pep; but her cabin was stifling. One noontime in desperation she seized her scissors to make cutoffs of her oldest jeans. But at the last second she changed her mind at the sight of white legs that hadn't had a chance to tan.

She moaned to Laurie, "If only we had a pool!"

"I'd push the mothers in, and grandmothers too,"

Laurie answered, lifting limp curls from her neck. "Thank goodness we'll have our vacation next month, Ernie and me. We'll spend it at the beach."

The beach sounded great to Sis, but she didn't want a vacation. "Who'll take your place here?" she asked.

"Who cares?" said Laurie.

Unlike the adults, the children hardly noticed the heat. They were burning with a different fire—horse show fever.

Lee had put Sis in charge of entries for Windy Hill. This meant tricky decisions, depending on how many parents could or would haul trailers, among other conditions. Half the kids wanted to enter the same classes on the same horses, which naturally was impossible. They disregarded entry fees, inadequate clothes, all competition, and their own and the horses' endurance. They argued, each claiming Sis for an ally. Patty alone refused to go, to Sis's relief. On the other hand Melissa, the small redhead, was desperate to go, if it was only to groom. "I'll even wash *tails*!" she kept repeating.

"It's always this way near show time," her mother told Sis with a resigned sigh.

Sis understood. Back home, when her coach took her along to shows, she'd burned with the same fever.

On this Monday, after their last class, her group had gathered midway down the aisle of Gull's barn, where it was coolest. Lee evidently had gone home. Bud had disappeared with Anita Pickett. Manuel had vanished, which he did so quietly that one seldom missed him.

Sis sat on the ground with the children, her back to the wall opposite Gull's stall. In the dim light, she peered at the Windy Hill entry form smeared by grubby fingers.

Turned to the jumper section, she mumbled aloud. "Jumpers, Novice, No, he's past that. . . . Jumpers, Ladies, maybe; they won't score manners. . . . Mm, let's see. . . . Ah, Open Jumpers! What's the purse?"

"Let *me* see." It was Bethie Nelson, an English rider. She breathed heavily over Sis's shoulder to see the page. "I could go in Equitation Twelve and Under, and in English Pleasure."

"Except your eq stinks," her brother said. "And you can't go in Pleasure because you lost your hunt cap."

"Shut up. I'll borrow one."

"Who from?"

Nobody volunteered, and Bethie mopped blue eyes as soft as her name. The mothers had a rule against borrowing.

"I'll try for high point junior," Bobby Nelson decided.

"He'll probably win it again," someone said glumly.

It was maddening to the girls that Bobby could win with little effort. Now one of them accused him, "You haven't even practiced."

"Can I help it," he retorted, "if I'm just naturally good—I mean great?"

"Ground him, Sis, ground him!"

As evening crept in, the group drifted away. Before she too left, Sis lingered for a last word with Gull. He came to the stall door, ghostly in the dusk. With one hand she pushed aside his foretop, then gently stroked his face. His eyes were dark pools, his nostrils warm velvet. His whiskers tickled her palm, and then his tongue curled out to lick the salty sweat on it. His breath had the good smell of grain.

"Good night, my horse," she said softly, and turned to go.

There stood a man, a few feet away. Her scream startled her. Then Bud's yellow hair gleamed faintly as he stepped closer. "What're you doin' here so late?" he asked.

"What are *you* doing?" she retorted. Bud in daytime was merely annoying, but it made her nervous to be here alone with him at night.

Maybe guessing her thought, he stood still and said, "Don't panic. I got other things on my mind better'n girls. Besides, I don't dig brown eyes and a round-type face."

About girls, Sis didn't believe him. She could have answered with some smart crack, but that might make him mad. I'll bet, she thought, he came to meet some girl, maybe Anita.

In the silence, she was conscious of horses stirring

and the taste of dust on the stagnant air. "I was just going," she said. "Uh, see you tomorrow."

"Mañana, like Manuel says."

As she walked away, her ears told her that Bud hadn't moved. It was a bit creepy knowing he was listening to her go, waiting until she'd left, for—what?

That night Sis disagreed with the kids who envied her for living here. Her room was an oven, even with the door open and light off. In pajamas, she lay on the cot, feeling trickles of sweat slide off her. Only an occasional rustle came from outdoors. There were raccoons and skunks in the woods, Jeff had told her, and of course squirrels, including hers, whom she'd named Whisk. She always recognized him by his crooked ear. He had grown bold enough to pick up the peanuts that she bought from Laurie and placed on the windowsill. There were owls, too, out there, and quail and woodpeckers. But tonight all were silent, maybe drained by the heat, as she was.

The rent horses had the best of it, she thought crossly. Turned out on the hill, they'd get whatever breeze stirred. Sometimes the pony Fury squealed up there when one of the others picked on him. His high voice was unmistakable. In looks, too, he stood out, being so tiny, a miniature Shetland. His sorrel coat verged on pink, and a cloud of white foretop screened his face.

For distraction, she thought about home. She ought to call or write. She could say she was fine, and loved her work; that Laurie let her use her washing machine, and had loaned her a reading lamp, and bossed her about meals. "You eat like you're retarded," Laurie'd scolded. "Pizza, pies, coffee! Get a ride to Blanche's now and then, and have a decent meal." Sis had done that a couple of evenings, but on the whole she preferred the privacy of her cabin after a day crowded by people. It was luxury to eat her snack in peace, throw off her clothes, and read herself to sleep.

Planning her letter home, she'd say the Ashbys were real nice to her. Jeff sometimes brought his mother, though each had a car. He'd chat while Sis worked, until Lee's sharp eyes parted them like a knife cutting butter.

But her folks mustn't get the wrong idea about Jeff. It was just that she needed someone to talk to. Everybody here was too young or too old or too busy. Except the barn boys, and for Manuel she'd have to learn Spanish though his English was improving a good deal. Poor Manuel, he moved about dreamily, listening to his little tinny radio. It hung inside his shirt, tuned always softly to Mexican music.

This whole picture didn't sound very exciting, Sis realized. But at home they wouldn't care about Gull, who was so exciting and so beautiful. If only they knew how marvelous it was when a person and a horse had a thing going between them. With some surprise, she was aware that she didn't really dread thinking about her dad. He seemed far away, his activities dwarfed by hers. She wondered if after all she'd blame him too much for his real estate deal without fully understanding it. Mimi did pressure him a lot, like for a new car, new clothes, entertaining . . . though of course nothing really excused cheating a client.

Unable to sleep, Sis got up and leaned from her window. The freshness above the creek was heavenly. It was only a step out onto a fork of the big tree. Lovely out here, the smell of bay, and of damp ferns below. Through the leaves overhead she glimpsed a sliver of moon, frail among stout golden stars.

A dog howled in the distance, and she hoped it wasn't one of the strays gone wild that Lee had told her about. They roamed the hills and attacked young calves, lambs, foals, anything, because they were starving. Ranchers shot them on sight. Horrible, she thought, and wished she hadn't heard about them.

She stepped up higher, where three horizontal branches joined the tree trunk to form a level place. Stretched out on it, she looked down, but couldn't see the water, only hear it. She did see the whole area, though, across the roof of her cabin. A light seemed to glow above Gull's barn, but so faintly that she might be dreaming it. She squinted to see it better, in vain. If it was real, it had to be coming through the skylight in Lee's storeroom. But he'd hardly be there this late. He must have forgotten earlier to switch it off.

After an interval, she grew uncomfortable on the rough tree bark, and climbed down in to bed. The room was still hot, and she wished there were some way to camp out. Then inspiration struck.

"Very clever," she said aloud. "Congratulations, Sis. You'll have a reason to ask Jeff over, because what's a carpenter's helper for? To build a treehouse, of course."

FIVE

On the Wednesday before the Windy Hill schooling show, Jeff brought lumber for the treehouse.

Leading Gull from the ring, Sis joined him where he was unloading lengths of boards from a flatbed truck below her cabin. She had waited to school until evening, hoping in vain to cool off. But now she was too elated to care about heat. "Oh, Jeff, you should have seen him jump! Like a—a bird!"

"A sea gull?"

She giggled. "I never saw a sea gull jump. But you know the stone wall we built?"

"His mental hazard?"

"Yes. Well, we had a little argument at it, and I won. Then, after he gave in, he was perfect over it, *perfect*! Twice!" She stroked Gull's sweaty neck.

"Want to show me?" Jeff asked, glancing toward the ring.

"I'd love to, but—no, we better not. He did it so well at the end, and other jumps, too; it just wouldn't be right to ask for more now. I want him to learn that when he goes well, he gets rewarded with a rest. When he goes badly, we have to keep at it."

She wasn't sure Jeff understood. But Lee did, and he approved her schedule for Gull: four days a week a pleasure ride, alone or in company; twice a week schooling, as short as possible; Mondays off, since she was busiest then, replacing either Bud or Manuel.

Jeff was looking at her as if she were a little nutty as she stood dripping beside her dripping horse.

"I'm going to give him a bath," she said. "Would you hold him a second?"

He took the rein, and she struggled from her boots, gasping with the effort, then rolled up her jeans. She tugged off her hunt cap, one of Lee's musts when schooling. "Whew, what a relief! Did it leave a mark?"

"Right across your forehead. Look, just to speed things up, I'll help you with Gull's bath."

Stripping off his shirt, Jeff tossed it in the truck. "I brought some fresh clothes," he said, "so later we can go eat at Blanche's."

"Why not?" Sis called back on her way to the washrack. She didn't want to appear thrilled.

Jeff caught up with her. Misunderstanding, he said, "I'd take you some place nicer, but Blanche's is close. I thought you'd want to get started building while there's daylight.''

Hobbling barefoot, she muttered, ''There'll be a half moon.''

What a dumb thing to say! Would he take it that she sat staring at the moon every night, dying for a date or something? She had barely enough composure to keep out of Gull's way.

The washrack was a cement floor with a drain and hitching post. While Jeff aimed the hose—partly at her—Sis soaped and scrubbed Gull, and used the scraper after each rinse. Rivulets of sweat and dust trickled off him, leaving his coat silvery. His hoofs shone. Drops twinkled on his eyelashes. Sis knew he was enjoying himself, especially when he reached for the hose nozzle and sucked in great gulps. Suddenly, catching her and Jeff off guard, he gave a mighty shake that showered them both and sent rainbow-hued bubbles soaring. Then, as if to share the joke, he raised his head and let out a boisterous neigh. The private horses answered from the barns, the rent horses from the hill so that for a few moments the shadowy valley echoed with whinnying.

''But look!'' The shriek was Sis's.

''What?''

She peered within inches of Gull's rump. ''Dapples! They're coming out on him!''

Jeff laughed. ''You make it sound like measles.''

''Won't he be gorgeous!'' she cried. ''I hoped—but I wasn't sure. . . . See, this is the first real bath I've given him. The dapples couldn't show up through all his old dirt.'' She was plucking at her soaked shirt.

"Take it off,'' Jeff said.

"My shirt? I would,'' she lied, "only the boys or Lee'd be sure to turn up.''

"Mine's off,'' Jeff persisted.

She looked at his tanned, muscled torso and mumbled, "That's different.''

"How so?'' He was grinning down at her in that teasing way that always panicked her. Loosing Gull's rope, she led him off, and heard Jeff's laugh behind them.

It was past eight when they reached Blanche's, and past nine when they came out. Sis sank back in the borrowed truck and yawned hugely.

"None of that, girl,'' Jeff warned. "We have work to do if you want that treehouse.''

"We don't have to finish it tonight,'' she said. "Remember, with school out there've been little monsters racing around all day. Plus, we're preparing for Windy Hill. Plus, the vet came to check Hurricane's hock, and it has to be soaked twice a day. Plus, Mrs. Pickett follows me around and never, ever stops talking. Is she nosy! And there's acres of tack to clean before Sunday. Then tomorrow, guess what?''

"It's your day off?''

"Very funny. Tomorrow's Grandma Day.''

"My gosh,'' Jeff said fervently as he braked in front of the cabin.

In old clothes again, they worked on into the night, at last cooler. Using Lee's ladder, Jeff passed up boards to Sis on the tree's natural platform. When they had the whole stack there they had to quit, for it was too dark to use a saw. A couple more hours' work should finish the job, they figured as they climbed down.

"Then we'll have a housewarming," Sis said.

"There's a better way," Jeff told her. "Have the housewarming first, and put the guests to work. How's that for a dirty trick?"

Sis heard him chuckle beside her. His face was only a light blur as they stood by the truck.

She didn't want him to leave, and said fast, "Thank you for all your help, and for dinner and everything. You were really swell to take so much trouble, and time, and, I mean . . ." Her words trailed off. In the sudden silence, she heard Whisk exploring the new boards above.

"I had fun," Jeff said.

"You did? I'm glad."

"Then I'm glad too." By his tone, he was smiling.

Helplessly, Sis listened to him open the truck door. Then in a rush she blurted, "We haven't said good night."

He turned back, and her heart started to thump. His breathing came nearer, and the glimmer of his shirt. His hand was on her shoulder. He was going to kiss her.

Instead, he said gruffly, "Come back in a year." Moments later, his motor roared, tires spurted gravel, and he was gone.

Sis smiled, while one hand crept to the shoulder he'd touched. Her hand lingered there, and her smile lingered also. Raising her warm face, she said to Whisk, "He wanted to kiss me, I know he did, but he thinks I'm too young." For dreamy minutes she stood listening to the sound of the truck dwindling smaller and smaller into the night.

Grandma Day began next morning with the arrival of two carloads of ladies. With cries of "This way, girls!" they hurried to the rent horses. They didn't wear jeans, but odd-shaped trousers and an assortment of blouses, shade hats, and hiking boots. They also wore smiles that were somehow contagious.

Manuel was a slave to the twittering group. At Lee's direction, he helped each one onto a horse, handed her the reins, and adjusted the stirrups. It made no difference to them which horse they rode; they had blind faith in Lee's judgment. All had ridden before at some time, but as one laughingly put it, "We forget everything! Now, Manuel, this is Tornado I'm on, si?"

"Si, señora." Manuel had just given the same answer to the same question asked by another grandma. In fact, whatever they said he answered with "Si, señora" and his nice smile. He hadn't exchanged so many smiles since Grandma Day last month.

At last they filed out, led by Lee who wouldn't trust the responsibility to anyone else. Having scheduled no lessons for this morning, he'd told Sis to follow the group. She thought it might be good experience for Gull.

At the trail markers beyond the bridge, Lee paused and turned to his charges, calling, "Shall we take Redwood Trail, or are you ladies game for Hill Trail?"

With daring words, they voted for the hill trail.

Before long their cries of "Wait!" and "Go on!" drifted back down to Sis. But luckily the horses recognized their own names, and obeyed Lee's voice as if they were riderless. He knew without looking back which ones were causing trouble. Once he hollered over a shoulder, "Git up there, Lightning! Just whack him, Mrs. Olsen, show him who's boss."

The answer floated down, "Oh, dear, I'm afraid he already knows."

Later, Lee warned, "Not so fast, Mrs. McCauley. Whirlwind in front of you's fixing to kick."

This morning everything pleased Sis. She was reliving last night, even while she told herself to forget it. So, she'd almost been kissed—maybe. So what? "Pay attention to now," she said, and dismounted to pick up sunglasses somebody'd dropped.

Up ahead, Lee halted the group and called, "Keep whatever it is, Sis, till we stop at Half Way Point. One of these days I'll put on a sale of all the things these ladies drop." The ladies tittered, and after some maneuvering rode on.

Half Way Point was a meadow between gentle hills.

At the riders' approach, a meadowlark shot up from the grass. Madrone trees, with their orange bark, gave dappled shade, and white blossoms of the buckeye trees smelled sweet.

The grandmas snapped pictures of one another and of the valley below. They exclaimed over the buttercups and blue lupin, and praised Sis for how well she managed Gull. Actually, he'd given her no trouble this morning beyond a little impatience. She knew it was Lee who deserved the praise, for his mount was a half-broke mare that he rode so expertly she appeared smooth.

From experience, Lee allowed only a five-minute rest. Homeward bound, he made sure no horse got by him, though some wanted to hurry. Part way down, he had to lead a timid rider whose horse, she claimed, was being very naughty. All were triumphant on reaching the stables again, where Manuel helped them dismount. After prolonged goodbyes they headed, rather stiffly, for the Wagon. One called, "My treat, girls!" and another, "Me first for the little girls' room!" What fun they had, Sis thought, and to Bud who sneered, "When I'm that old, just bury me," she snapped, "Sure. Alive."

That leisurely morning was a contrast to the afternoon and to the two remaining days before Windy Hill. Sis discovered how much more easily she could cope with children than with their parents. The first pestered her only for added schooling, the second with constant interruptions. One mother was offended when Sis told her child *never* to chew gum in the show ring. A father was mortified when, ''helping'' his daughter, he put spurs on her backwards.

Of course Sis referred important decisions to Lee, who remained cool through all activity, though busier than usual. He allowed her to use his desk and telephone in the office for checking details connected with the show. From there, she stole occasional visits with Laurie next door.

Gull was doing well. He'd put on weight since she'd been feeding him grain, which she bought through Jeff. Her rides, due to heat and added work, were mostly at night, under the ring's lights.

Bud's offer to bet against Gull at Windy Hill was an insult. ''He won't even be in the money,'' Bud said.

''Of course he will! I mean he easily might. Why wouldn't he?''

''Because he'll throw fits. Five bucks?''

''I can't bet,'' Sis said. ''I'm saving to buy him his own grooming tools.''

''Chicken! Well, some sucker'll bet on him.'' Bud grinned. ''Someone who don't know him.''

Sunday morning a knock on Sis's door wakened her. There stood Melissa, asking, ''Am I late, Ms.?'' Her voice, always shrill, seemed unbearable at this hour.

Sis groaned. ''It's not even daylight! But come in. Who brought you?''

''My mom,'' said Melissa. ''I told her we better be

here about half past four. Don't you love to get up in the dark and see the stars?''

It was sort of fun at that—once you were awake. It reminded Sis of past horse show mornings, of trips over snowy miles much longer than today's drive would be.

While she dressed, Melissa asked her, ''Would you like a roast beef sandwich with pickles and mustard? My mom brought some.''

''Thanks, but it's kind of early for lunch,'' Sis answered. ''I'll see how my stomach is later.'' Right now it was shuddering.

''My mom thought,'' said Melissa, ''that if I eat a good lunch I might not fall off today.''

''That's an idea,'' Sis hedged.

Within minutes, plans materialized. Headlights appeared as families arrived. Hay was stuffed in trailer mangers, tack in tack compartments, clothes in cars and station wagons. Bud prepared to haul one trailer, several parents others. Lee climbed behind the wheel of the ranch's four-horse van. Sis loaded Gull in it, next to his stablemate Twinkle. This would be Mrs. Ashby's first show, in which she'd agreed to enter an Amateur Pleasure class, ''just for fun.'' Gracious even at this hour, she took charge of Sis's boots and hunt cap, jacket, shirt, and breeches.

Stars had dimmed when the caravan started, leaving only Manuel, with his radio music. As the van lumbered out over the ranch road, Sis stood inside it between two pairs of horses riding head to tail. She liked the rumbling and creaking, and the flash of horses' eyes when the lights of the Junction, then of other towns, beamed in through the vents. Two of the horses were eating, those with mangers. The other two pawed now and then, and their stomachs growled. They'd eat on arrival, not being in early classes.

Sis felt the van begin the climb to Windy Hill, and presently turn in to the grounds and lurch to a stop. When Lee let her out, the first sun rays greeted her. Friends waved to "the Tanbark bunch," but didn't take time to visit. All hurried to unload, to unzip leg and tail wraps, to saddle, to exercise in the ring before the show would start. The ring was not enclosed but open, comfortable for most horses. The weather, too, was comfortable so far, with the expected breeze.

It was the first time Sis had ridden Gull in such a crowd, and both were a bit nervous. But so were other horses and riders, she saw; even trainers. Lee, standing at the rail, was scolding Bethie Nelson for taking the wrong lead. Anita Pickett had collided with another girl. And a heavy man on a pinto was trying without success to jump a practice fence. When Sis passed him a second time and heard him curse his horse, she recognized Karl Kramer. Gull shied from them as if the sight and sound repelled him as much as it did her.

After that, Gull's tension increased, especially when the loudspeaker came on strong. "Clear the ring," it bellowed, and plainly Gull was eager to obey. Sis made him exit slowly and walk back to the van. At least he'd been exercised. Now he could relax while she watered and groomed him. Then she'd go help her English riders; she'd change; and maybe, she'd eat something.

As time for the Ladies' Jumpers approached, she kept busy coaching. She was rather glad that for once Bobby Nelson wasn't likely to win high point junior. A bulldog-faced rider from another stable had drawn ahead. Mrs. Ashby showed and didn't place, but claimed she was having fun anyway. She looked tired, but surely, Sis thought, this was better therapy for her than anything else. Surprisingly, Melissa, far from falling off, won her first blue ribbon and wept with joy.

"What's that lady doing?" a student asked Sis. The woman she pointed out carried a sort of broom handle with a cup at one end.

"She's been hired to test horses for drugs," Sis explained. "She'll pick any horse among the winners, and when it leaves the ring, she'll have its rider take it to an empty stall. They'll wait there till the horse goes to the bathroom, and she'll catch some of its urine in the cup. She'll seal the sample and send it to a lab for analyzing."

Wide-eyed, the student asked, "And the sample might show that the horse was doped? Then what?"

"Then the owner's in big trouble," Sis answered. "He's fined and grounded and so on." Her mind was not on this conversation. It was a relief to see Lee arrive. He handed her her number, checked his watch, and said, "Jocks up."

Before she even reached the warm-up area, she knew Gull was still on edge. He mouthed his bit, shaking back flecks of foam. He humped his back. He twitched his ears. Willing herself to unwind him, she loosened every part of her body. She hummed. She gave and took with the snaffle. But she too started when the loudspeaker shouted, "Jumpers next, ladies to ride." Shortly, as if everyone were deaf, it repeated, "Ladies' Jumpers, you're next."

At the ring gate, Karl Kramer was helping a girl onto his pinto. Sis looked away, but not quickly enough to avoid seeing bloody streaks on the pinto's sides. She whispered to Gull, "You'll *never* belong to that man!"

With Lee at her stirrup, she studied the performance of each rival ahead of her. None so far had gone clean, though a young woman who rode with superb timing scored only one half fault. Yet the course wasn't tricky. No stone wall, thank goodness. Although Sis was ready, the announcer's call surprised her: "Number seventy-one, Sea Gull, owned by the Tanbark Ranch, ridden by Sis Reynolds."

"In you go," said Lee.

Sis collected Gull and walked him through the open gate. The buzz of voices dropped. As she trotted a circle before the first jump, she vaguely saw faces along the rail and smelled tanbark. Then she was headed for the brush, holding Gull to a canter instead of the gallop he wanted.

Over the brush. Picket fence next—those points like

teeth! Slow down, that's better. All right! We're over that one too with no faults. Hear his good pounding strides and his blowing. The pump of his shoulders and thrust of hindquarters say he could gallop ten miles cross-country, and laugh at my weight on his back!

Now, ready for the crossed bars—okay, still clean. Now turn—hey, are you trying to buck or what? Here comes the panel—beautiful, but no need to jump it that big! A voice shouts "Keep it up!" Reverse now, change leads, and back over the same fences.

Sis felt a great glow as the glimpsed unexpected victory, or at worst a jump-off.

But past the far turn, Gull grabbed the bit and put on speed. *Hold back, hold back!* She slowed him, not enough. As if in fun, he charged the remaining fences. A front rap, a pole down, a whole fence down! Somebody guffawed, "Timber!" And going out, to complete the shambles, a real buck!

Outside, Lee said, "I've seen better."

Sis lacked the breath to answer. She nodded, fighting tears. She'd worked so hard with Gull, hoped for so much! Oh, gosh, why hadn't she held him?

"Get down," Lee ordered. "Cool him and tie him at the van. And don't be a sore loser. Your horse enjoyed himself at any rate. Look at him."

Gull was wearing the funniest expression, nearly sheepish.

After a moment, Lee asked sharply, "Have you been graining him?"

"A little bit," Sis mumbled toward her boots.

When she looked up, Lee was frowning. "I see," he said.

But what he saw seemed to be not all bad. He went on, "Well, I didn't bring him here to play. Of course, we can take that out of him, but not in time for the Open class. I'll go scratch."

"But your entry fee!"

He shrugged. "Better to lose a few bucks than to ruin a good prospect."

On her way to the van, Sis saw Bud with a group of pals. He grinned at her. So the creep had won his bet against Gull. "Thanks, sweetheart!" he yelled.

Not caring who heard, she yelled back, "Drop dead!"

SIX

"Howdy," Sis began her second letter to Marion and Eve. It was Monday evening, a week after Windy Hill. "I should have answered you both sooner, but I've been busy. Also having fun. Also learning. There's a million things to learn in a place like this when you plan to make horses your career."

She paused to think about Gull. Her sisters wouldn't understand, but she had to try. On her cot, she shifted position and continued.

"Gull listens for my step in the morning, and nickers under his breath at me, and lips my hands. For such a big horse to be so loving is kind of sweet. Of course, he knows I'll feed him. No more grain though, it sends him! It made him so high at Windy Hill that he acted like a two-year-old. Physically, too, he's improved with regular work. And his jumping is getting consistent."

But it was silly to go on about Gull.

"Marion, you asked me about Lee. Well, I've grown to really respect him. He's not exactly cuddly, but he's fair, and a terrific worker. It bothers him that the barn boys don't work harder, but he says these two are better than others he's hired. Manuel's shy, and seems to need Bud's help. He's an illegal alien, Bud says, scared the police will deport him home to Mexico.

"Back to Lee. He plans to build a home here, and to add more box stalls and a hot walker. He must be lonely sometimes, being single, but I think he's happy. He acts happiest when he drives the rent horses down every morning when the sun just touches the hilltops, not yet the valley. Then he rides bareback, and he whistles. I see him because I'm out early too, on my way to Gull. I like that time, cool and all still before the new day.

"Lee wasn't mad at me when I clobbered the course at Windy Hill. After the class I acted like a brat, and chewed my nails all the way home. I must have looked terrible, because Lee gave me the next day off. What was fabulous, he said I should ride this next weekend at the Sequoia County fair. Boy, did that boost my morale! He said Gull was a good prospect. Naturally, he knows darn well I'll work twice as hard now.

"Did I tell you he had an awful row with Laurie over her smoking? He ordered her to quit it 'for the last time.' I have no idea what'll happen, but I'd sure miss her if she left."

Sis contemplated another subject, then tackled it.

"You wrote that Jeff sounded nice. He is nice—that's all. I mean, he's practically middle-aged, and most likely has thousands of dates. The more the merrier.

"Guess I've rambled on enough. It's getting late, and I still want to finish a super mystery story. How's Mimi? Say 'Hi' from me." Sis considered sending a message to her dad, but couldn't bring herself to do it.

Next morning, Lee took the letter to mail when he drove Bud to Berkeley. Bud always got a ride out on his day off; at night a friend brought him back. Manuel preferred to spend his free Mondays at the ranch. Now, as on most Mondays, Lee planned to do some business in town. Meantime, Sis was to substitute for Bud, to teach two classes, and to turn half the rent horses back on the hill. They'd had a full day yesterday and wouldn't all be needed today.

Her second class was at eleven, and she had to resist the urge to cut it short. The ring was stuffy, hotter than outside. It was good to step into her cabin at noon. She'd take a break until Lee's pickup rattled past, getting home. Collapsed on her cot, she daydreamed about the coming county fair.

But an odd sound kept interrupting her dream. Ordinarily she ignored the horses' voices, but with Lee and Bud both away—

She sat up, conscious that the sound had been going

on for some time. Darn, what was wrong with Fury? The pony'd been all right when she'd turned him out earlier.

Next second his frantic neighing electrified her. At the same time, a child's shriek split the quiet noon.

Sis snatched open her door. For a moment an appalling sight paralyzed her. "No—they'll kill him!" she screamed. "Keep out! *Keep out*!"

Flying, she made for the lowest pasture corner. Three dogs surrounded Fury there—a large shepherd, a smaller one, and a yellow dog nearly Fury's size. Together and in turn they were attacking, darting at his head, his belly, his hindquarters. The noise was ghastly. Snarls mingled with the pony's neighs and with the shrieks of the little girl about to crawl through the fence to Fury.

Sis flung herself on the child, who fought her desperately while sobbing, "Save the pony, they're hurting it! They're *hurting* it!"

"Shut up!" Sis yelled at her, but didn't dare let her go. Holding her, she couldn't climb the fence herself. Both were gasping with horror at the shambles a few feet away. Tears gushed down Sis's face as a voice, maybe hers, screamed "Lee! Manuel! *Somebody*!"

Backed into the corner, Fury was weakening. Blood smeared his coat and reddened his long white tail, and stained the sweat running off him. His little stick legs twisted and tripped in the dirt and manure, ready to snap. His foretop was no longer a white cloud, but a thick red mass that rose and fell as he went to his knees and up again, over and over. He seemed to be bowing and bowing, in a nightmare that must soon have an end too gruesome to watch.

The dogs lunged and snarled, bit flesh and hung on, and fell back to lunge again. They too were splashed with blood, but not their own. All three were thin, shaggy brutes. The yellow one seemed the leader, his growls deep and savage. The big shepherd worked methodically to hamstring Fury. The small one attacked with agile springs, her barks as vicious as her teeth that snapped shining in the sunlight.

Fury was silent now, except to pant. Still he struggled, rolling in the dust and the noise and the stench. The other horses watched from the hillside, but none came to his help.

Sis couldn't stand it any longer. Loosing the child, she shouted at her, "Don't move, you hear?" She looked about wildly, saw a stick and seized it and was halfway up the fence.

At that moment Lee's voice thundered, "Get off that fence!" His pickup skidded to a stop beside her. In one jump he jerked her down. Then he raced towards his storeroom. Speed blurred his long legs and brought him back in seconds—with a gun.

Sis covered her eyes and dragged the little girl backwards.

The shot cracked out. There was a gurgling grunt and the thump of a falling body. When she looked, the yellow dog lay dead next to Fury. The other dogs were streaking away. Lee fired again, but they were out of range.

Lee's eyes on Fury were grim. "Looks about finished," he said. He set the loaded gun down through the fence, then climbed in after it.

"Are you—are you—" Sis couldn't manage, *Are you going to shoot Fury*? She didn't want to look at Fury, and when she did look, she had to turn away. Things began to go around and around. She sat down fast because the ground was tilting. Then she heard Lee unload his gun.

Without looking at her, he began, "Watch Fury while I—" He glanced over. "Oh. Well, I'll watch him. You run and call Doctor Emory. In my office. The number's on the phone. If you can't reach Doc, call the other number, Doctor Nesbit. Tell 'em they may have to put a horse down. You know what I mean?"

"Yes. Kill him," Sis said faintly.

"And take that kid, whoever she is." Lee bent over Fury again, and Sis fled, pulling the little girl along.

Her heart continued to pound while she called both vets, then the child's home. A brother said he'd be right over. "Stay here, your brother's coming," she told the child, and turned to leave. But she stopped and dragged a tissue from her pocket. "Here, dry your face." Her own face was salted stiff with tears and sweat. Seeing the child still sobbing, she said, "I'll wait with you."

It was a short wait before they heard the approach of

the boy on a bicycle. Sis left. Not running this time, she headed back to Fury. "Coward," she whispered to herself. "Don't—when you see him—no matter what—don't you pass out."

"He's in shock," Lee told her, "but the vet'll want him moved. I'm going to open the pasture gate and drive in. Several together, we can lift him onto the pickup bed. Which vet's coming?"

"Doctor Nesbit."

"Darn. That's the woman." Lee scowled, looking more like himself—but not much more.

His lunch break over, Manuel showed up. He appeared to take the disaster without surprise. Most likely he'd seen death more than once. He looked at the fallen pony and in his gentle way said only, "*Se muere.*"

"Get a shovel and bury the dog," Lee ordered him, with motions. And he said harshly, maybe to himself, "It's the bums who turn dogs loose that oughtta be shot."

The vet arrived next, an assured young person, trim in her white coveralls. She requested a blanket and helped slide it under Fury. Sis didn't look at him. One at each corner, they carried it, taut, to the pickup.

"Let's get him to a box stall without jarring," Doctor Nesbit directed. "Then I'll need hot water. When I've cleaned those wounds—we'll see."

Sis listened, her eyes stretched wide. What did "we'll see" mean?

"If you want to save him," the vet went on—

"Do what you can." Lee spoke as if it didn't matter, but his next words gave him away "I raised him myself from birth when the mother died. He turned fifteen last March . . ."

Evidently Doctor Nesbit got the message. She said briskly, "I'll sedate him first. Then he'll need a shot of penicillin, and a tetanus shot. When I sew him up, I'll want a flashlight and someone to hold it. Let's go."

Any other time Sis would have grinned at the sight of Lee bossed by this slight, cool young woman. Now she was half relieved when he sent her to cope with the clients arriving. Before moving off, she watched the pickup inch its way toward Manuel's barn. Like an ambulance, she thought. Manuel and Doctor Nesbit walked beside it. No, it was like a hearse.

That afternoon was unreal to Sis. At her chores, which included Bud's, she spoke as little as possible, evading people and their questions. Her head ached, she guessed, from the strain of trying to determine what was going on in Manuel's barn. He and Lee had stayed inside it, as far as she knew, and Doctor Nesbit's car was still by the pasture fence.

"Are you sick, Sis?" a youngster asked.

"Just tired."

"You look funny. How come?"

Sis longed to be alone, to take some aspirin and a shower. Even more, she longed for news of Fury, but hadn't the courage to go ask. Only in the late afternoon, when she saw the vet's car still there, did she decide that the worst hadn't happened. If Doctor Nesbit had given the fatal injection—euthanasia, they called it—she would have left.

Sis had fed all the indoor horses and cleaned box stalls when she heard Lee's pickup start. That meant he was going to feed those turned out. Now another motor started. The vet's! Sis stepped outside, and cringed from the still-bright glare.

Lee was gray-faced. "Got 'em all fed?" he asked.

"Yes." Pause. "Fury—?"

"He'll need luck. We'll know in a couple of days. Manuel's going to take care of him. But it wouldn't hurt you to lend a hand. You won't break, you know, just by looking at a sick horse." Lee raised his hat to wipe his forehead.

Sis felt her face redden. He was right, of course. What good would she be around a stable if sights like today's made her sick?

"Have you mucked out?" he asked.

"Yes, I've done everything except ride Gull."

"Then don't. The shape you're in, you'd do him more harm than good. He'd take advantage of you. Longe him instead. But first, help me feed in pasture. Manuel has to be with Fury when he comes to, so he don't fight and bust his stitches. I doubt there's any fight left in the little guy, but I'll go along with what Doctor Nesbit wants. I've got to say she did a fine job."

For a woman, he means, Sis thought, and hoped Doctor Nesbit would send a huge bill. Head throbbing, she opened the pasture gate, closed it behind Lee, and with her pitchfork climbed onto the pickup's bed to toss out the hay at intervals.

The valley was darkening when at last she was free, after a final check on Gull. But on the way to her cabin she stopped at the entrance to Manuel's barn. The only sound inside was the munch of horses finishing their supper. Mixed with the smell of feed, an antiseptic odor tinged the air. From where she stood, the stall doors gave no clue to Fury's whereabouts. She called Manuel's name softly, received no answer, and walked in.

Along the aisle her sneakers were soundless, but she imagined the horses could hear the heartbeats under her dusty T-shirt. She passed several rumps, then stopped and stared into a stall. After a moment, she half smiled to herself. Somehow the picture reminded her vaguely of a Christmas card, the Bethlehem scene with animals at the manger. Side by side, just touching, Fury and Manuel were asleep. She tiptoed away.

A quick trip to her cabin for a flashlight and money. She'd decided to buy Manuel his supper, along with hers. She'd eat in the stall with him, since Lee felt she ought to help. What did he think she'd been doing all day—resting?

At the Wagon, Laurie asked the same question, less politely, after Sis described her day. Laurie went on, "I heard some noise at noon, but I was filling an order and couldn't stop. Then this afternoon it did seem awful quiet. I was glad for Ernie, him havin' to sleep daytimes. But I'm surprised Lee'd have that lady vet. He never would before. If he thinks men are superior, where are his wonder boys now? One playin' lover in town, the other snorin'. *We're* doin' the work . . . suckers. Say'' —a wicked gleam sparked Laurie's black eyes—''how about if you and me go on strike? More pay, less hours, or else. What do you say, kid?''

''I say no.'' Sis laughed, and left with two brown bags. The jumbo burgers and french fries inside them smelled great.

They tasted great, too, she and Manuel agreed by sign language. A full moon had lit her way to the barn; now the flashlight helped. It showed in Manuel's face a touching gratitude.

And it showed Fury. He hadn't moved, except to open eyes veiled by pain. Of course, by now the sedative would have worn off. Sis ached to put her arms around him, but didn't dare. Numerous black stitches crisscrossed his poor stomach. Others laced his hind legs. His lovely foretop had been cut off; it would have covered more stitches. Merthiolate painted his wounds a shocking red. As Lee had said, he was far from fighting—nearer, Sis thought, to giving up.

She made eating motions to ask whether Fury had eaten. Manuel held out one cupped hand, and now he scooped another palmful of oats from a can beside him. When he offered it, Fury lifted his head and lipped a few grains, but the effort was too much. With a groan, he lay back again. His eyes on Sis begged for something.

She searched for the answer, but Manuel found it

first. "*Agua*." And he added, to show off his English, "Water."

There was still water in the bucket Lee had left, but evidently Fury was too weak to stand up and drink.

Together they raised his fore-end gingerly and tilted the bucket enough for him to reach water. He drank slowly, for many minutes, and afterwards gave a deep sigh. So did Sis. She'd been terrified that he would tear some stitches.

She asked Manuel if he meant to sleep here.

He showed that he understood by lying down as he had before, next to Fury. One brown hand closed around a tiny hoof. Sis left him her flashlight.

In the dark aisle, she paused a few moments, listening. What she heard, very softly, was Mexican music. Bolder since she'd gone, Manuel tried his English on Fury. "You like, eh?"

That night she couldn't get to sleep, tired though she was. She kept seeing Fury in the stall, and the look he'd given her, pleading—for what? She'd thought it was just for water—but it could have been for something else. Maybe he wanted the final release from suffering. Lee had said, "He'll need luck." Doctor Nesbit had said, "We'll see." How long, Sis wondered, would they make Fury wait? Somewhere she'd read about a horse put down, "beyond the reach of pain and fear . . ." If Fury were human, he'd have a choice. It wasn't fair.

In tears, Sis burrowed under the pillow. But still she

smelled a trampled pasture, and heard the snarls, and saw dogs bait a blood-smeared pony who bowed and bowed almost to death.

SEVEN

LATER THAT NIGHT a car woke Sis, no doubt bringing Bud home. It passed again almost immediately on its way out.

The smell of lumber drifted in the window. It reminded her of the housewarming she and Jeff had planned, to finish the treehouse. Jeff's mother was due for another ride. Maybe he'd bring her. Heavens, he didn't know yet about Fury.

Sis sat up at thought of Fury. She wondered if Manuel really knew enough to follow Doctor Nesbit's orders—things like how to take Fury's temperature, to feed lightly, to help him turn or stand. And who was supposed to do Manuel's normal work? And how would they all get ready for the County Fair this weekend? It would be an overnight jaunt at that, because the drive took several hours, and they were to show early Sunday morning.

Falling back, she groaned, "Go away, everything. I just want to sleep." But she couldn't.

After a restless interval she crawled out onto the platform. Now in July the water beneath her was low. Except for its murmur, silence was absolute. Over her cabin's roof, she saw how the round moon whitened the valley and blackened the buildings. It dimmed a glow just apparent above Lee's storeroom. As once before, he'd forgotten to turn off his light. This time it must have been after he put his gun back. The thought of anything unusual next door to Gull made Sis uneasy. She decided to go see. A walk might help her sleep.

Dressed, she padded down the hill. It was eerie to be out in the black-and-whiteness and the total quiet.

Light came weakly from Gull's barn, and at the entrance she saw why: the door to Lee's storeroom was ajar. A sound inside halted her. Someone was there! Her pulse began to throb, faster and faster. She tried to swallow, and couldn't. She felt suffocated.

Should she run for Bud and Manuel—for Ernie? Ernie was at work. Laurie, then?

Before she could move, the storeroom door swung slowly wider. Petrified, she watched a man's arm appear—his shoulder—leg—until he stood fully in the light. It was Bud! Relief flooded her, and she called his name.

He jumped, and both together asked, "What're *you* doing here?"

She answered first. "I saw the light and came to investigate."

"Me too." He switched the light off and added, "The door was open."

She heard the door pulled shut, then the click of the lock. She thought of Lee's gun, but didn't mention it, only asked, "Was everything all right inside?"

"Sure, I guess so. Ol' Lee must be gettin' careless."

"He had too much on his mind today," Sis explained. "If you saw Manuel, you know about Fury."

"I haven't seen Manuel," Bud said. "I didn't stop at the trailer."

"He's not at the trailer. At least I don't think so. But—" Sis was growing confused.

Bud stepped closer. Once again, it made her nervous to be alone with him in the dark barn. She turned to Gull who loomed, ghostly, at the door. He nuzzled her as she stroked his neck, and the familiar feel of him reassured her enough to tell Bud about Fury.

"But," she ended, still puzzled, "how come you haven't been at your trailer?" She'd heard him come home quite a while ago.

After a moment, Bud answered, "I came here direct when I got home—if you have to know."

"Oh." Well, there was no point in standing here arguing at this time of night, or morning.

Bud agreed, saying, "Let's move it. Shall we go see Fury?"

A few minutes later they were standing at Fury's stall. They heard radio music, but could see nothing.

Bud asked, low, "Want me to get a flashlight?"

"No," Sis whispered. "Listen. You can hear them both breathe. Let's not wake them." She finished, clumsily, "Good night."

Inches away, Bud asked, "Could I walk you home . . . or something?"

"No. Oh, no. Thanks." And she scurried out into the welcome moonlight.

Her cabin felt absurdly safe to her, considering the door had no lock and the window no curtain. In bed again, she told herself it was silly to be afraid of Bud. He'd never tried anything with her. She needed more experience with boys. Just the same, she didn't trust him. His sudden interest in Fury, and his attempt to please her, struck her as phony. And then, if it was true that when he came home he'd gone directly to Lee's storeroom, he would have been there alone fifteen minutes or more. Doing what? Poking around, she guessed. Lee had said he kept nothing of value there. Still, she'd better remind him to be more careful about locking up. Poor man, she hoped he was getting some sleep, after the Fury business. He'd be sure to turn up extra early tomorrow. "To*day*," she moaned, rolling over.

Lee did arrive early, but Sis didn't know it. She had slept right through her alarm. Skipping breakfast, she ran to Fury's stall, and found Lee there.

The pony was up, looking unhappy but a little brighter than yesterday.

"His fever's down one degree," Lee said. "He ate a few mouthfuls just now, and drank. But . . . I don't know. . . .By the way, Bud told me that last night he found my storeroom open. I must have left it that way after I put my gun back. Did you notice?"

"No," Sis answered. "I guess I was too flustered. But—"

Impatient as always, he cut in, "No big deal. I just checked. The gun hadn't been touched. Now I gotta call Doctor Nesbit, and you get to work. You're late."

It annoyed Sis that Bud had been the one to tell Lee about the storeroom, making himself the hero, of course. He wouldn't have mentioned how long he was in there. She was further annoyed to find he'd fed Gull and cleaned the stall. She didn't want his favors. This morning, at her chores, she ignored him. Manuel, too, was working, since Fury didn't need constant attention.

Needed or not, he had it nearly all day. It seemed everyone knew his story, which grew with each repetition. Sis heard one version in which Fury, by himself, killed a dog twice his size, and chased half a dozen others away. Another version had it that Fury attacked some poor little lost dogs, and Lee heartlessly shot them.

"Prob'ly somebody's pets," Bethie Nelson said, blinking back tears. "Or maybe one of them was a seeing-eye dog."

Realism returned when Lee reported his talk with the sheriff. "Sheriff says there's more of these wild dogs running our hills here, killing livestock. So, anyone sees a stray, tell me.'' His steely gray eyes singled out Bethie. ''These dogs are *not* pets—not any more. They're dangerous.''

To Sis he went on, ''I heard from the parents of that child who was here. They know that if it hadn't been for you, she'd have crawled in with Fury, and the dogs likely would've turned on her.''

There were ''Oh's'' of horror, followed by compliments for Sis. Praise from the kids was nice; from Lee, it was fantastic. But then, frowning at the group, he asked, ''Well, do you aim to spend the day here talking?''

They did spend a good deal of it talking—to Fury. With furtive glee, they formed the Pony Sitters Club, and took turns waiting on Fury, petting him, tenderly brushing him, fanning off flies. All this between lessons and odd jobs. Sis saw that Manuel felt left out. When she said so to the kids, they made him an honorary club member, whether or not he knew it.

But the next day their attention to Fury slackened, by Lee's orders. They had to prepare for the County Fair.

There was the usual pre-show frenzy of unscheduled lessons; tack to clean; horses to trim, to bathe, to vacuum. Melissa did tails, a dime apiece. The shoer came, and made sparks fly and steam rise from the ping-ping on his anvil. Bud serviced cars, trailers, and the van. The two mothers going, Mrs. Nelson and Mrs. Murphy, planned happily for the weekend in the mountains. Besides them, there'd be three young ones: Melissa, Bobby, and Bethie Nelson; and four middle-aged ones: Sis, Bud, Anita, and Melissa's older brother, another redheaded Murphy. They were to camp on the fairgrounds, sleep in bedrolls around a fire, and cook there or eat in the 4-H tent.

On Friday, Lee announced he was staying. He wouldn't risk being gone while wild dogs roamed the area. And, he didn't want to leave Fury.

"Bud'll drive the van," he said, "with Gull and the Nelson horses. Murph will haul the other two. And you drivers watch out for logging trucks; any trouble, you're through hauling for me."

Sis wondered what Murph was like, having rarely seen him. He had outgrown his horse, and taken a summer job sandblasting. And naturally, she wondered and worried how Gull would perform. Just because he was going well here didn't mean he'd go well at the show.

"It's for your own sake you must behave," she told him that Friday afternoon in his stall. "Lee can't wait much longer for you to earn your keep. If you don't, then what?"

He must have caught the sadness in her tone, for he raised his head from the feed pan, his fine breedy head that she loved. Big deep eyes returned her love.

Leaning against his shoulder, she watched the motions of his jaw as he ate. She pressed one ear to his stomach, and heard it digesting. His coat smelled healthy. She must have brushed it a thousand strokes, and given him hundreds of other attentions, large and small. Spoiled him, maybe. She knew him so well! If she were blind, she'd recognize him among other horses, by his height, his neigh, his walk—oh, lots of ways. Just as he'd know her step in the dark any time. If he didn't prove to Lee soon—if *she* didn't prove. . . . It would be her fault if he lost this good home. He might go to a terrible one. . . . Her eyes smarted, and Gull wavered through her tears. "I'll die if he sells you," she whispered.

After the day's last lesson, she listened against her good sense to the children's descriptions of what the fair treats would include—a Ferris wheel, roller coaster, shooting gallery, burro baseball, chariot races, and the girl in spangles fired from a cannon.

"Gull will come apart," she said later that evening to Jeff. He'd brought his sleeping bag for her to take along, and invited her to dinner.

Nervous and depressed, she turned him down. She guessed his feelings were hurt, for in turn he hurt hers by saying, "I thought you had guts."

"I do—I mean, usually I do, but—" She was almost crying. "Oh, it'll be awful. With all that racket, Gull will blow sky high!"

"Not if you don't," Jeff argued.

"That's stupid." More likely true, she knew.

He left abruptly. She didn't care. She wanted to be alone. She wished she could stay home tomorrow.

Before going to bed, she scraped soap under her fingernails so she wouldn't bite them in her sleep. It was a trick she'd invented that sometimes worked.

A good sleep, overdue, improved her mood next morning. "I made a fool of myself over what may never happen," she said to Whisk. He cocked his crooked ear at her in surprise when she tugged the window shut. "No prowlers while I'm away," she told him through the glass.

Before the caravan left, Bud urged her to ride beside him in the van. He volunteered, "This time I'll bet *on* Gull."

"You expect me to bet against him?" she exclaimed.

"Only kidding. But somebody will, and I'll collect. I got a hunch Gull's gonna be lucky."

For that, she almost liked him. Still, she chose to travel inside the van. It was fun to watch the horses, and safer for them to be watched.

The stretch on the freeway was uneventful. But to Sis, mountain country was exciting, and she tried to recall what she'd read of this territory. It wasn't until arrival, however, after noon, that she was able to see and smell a logging community combined with a sprawling fair.

Bud backed the van skillfully into the designated parking space, and Sis ran to the horse show office. Today was local day, riders being from the area only, some of them obviously green. She had to dodge ponies, 4-H kids leading calves, a loose ewe with twin lambs, and sunburned crowds drifting from the Gay-way. From there too came screams and rifle shots, smells of cotton candy, and the taste of frying.

In the office, she stood in line to receive numbers, programs, and time schedules for the Tanbark bunch. Mrs. Nelson waved to her from another line where camping sites were being allotted. Sis laughed when, outside, Mrs. Nelson collided with a toddler blinded by the giant panda he clutched.

They'd been given a good site, shady, not too far from the rest rooms or the barns. It included a faucet, a trash can, a stone fireplace, and a wooden table with benches. But before they could enjoy it, they had to exercise, school, and feed their horses.

Sis put in several hours coaching, all that time riding Gull. It was her attempt to relax him. Though nervous at first—and no wonder—he finally began to tire. With others, she rode on the half-mile track, around the infield where the ring was located. Teams were playing burro baseball in the infield, which upset most horses; fortunately, the chariot races weren't scheduled until tomorrow. Sis refused to think about them. "We'll just do our best," she said to Gull when she put him away, "and, like Bud says, we may be lucky."

In camp with the kids, she could see why they spoke of this weekend as the high point of their year. The scene had a sort of romance. One by one, small fires twinkled in the deep blue shadows. Someone played a guitar in a nearby camp, and others sang. A smell strange to Sis intrigued her, and she asked what it was.

"It's witch hazel, a bush," Murph answered, seated next to her. "Some folks call it mountain misery. But the main smell around here is always the lumber mills. Reminds you of a carpenter's shop." And of Jeff, Sis thought.

They gorged on roast chicken, ears of corn, salads and pies from home. Meanwhile, they watched an ornate motor home maneuvering into another camp, like a great ship docking. It was followed by a gold Corvette. When the occupants of both stepped out, voices rose, with tipsy laughter. Among the voices, Sis recognized Karl Kramer's. She turned away in disgust.

"Something wrong, Freckles?" Murph asked her.

"Only a jerk I hate," she answered.

"Where? I'll kill him."

She laughed. "And if you call me Freckles, I'll kill you."

"Let's go to the Gayway," he suggested. Anita and Bud already had disappeared, and the younger ones were edging from the table.

Mrs. Murphy raised her voice. "Listen, children. Murph, you keep an eye on your sister and her friends. You're to be back by eleven, no later. You'll be up early tomorrow, and we don't want you half dead."

"Sometimes I don't want them on any terms," Mrs. Nelson said to her, and the two laughed together.

On the Gayway's rides, Sis screamed as loudly as

anyone. She threw rings, shot at targets, guessed weights, won an ash tray, laughed at the clowns, ate junk food, and saw the girl shot from the cannon. It was all a blast, and she and Murph didn't really mind that the three little Tanbark kids trailed them. But before eleven those three were worn out and had to be returned to camp.

There, Murph asked, "Now what? Back to the Gayway?" His red hair glowed by the dying fire.

"No, I've had it," Sis answered. "Let's just go see that the horses are okay."

They made their dark way to the barn around silent forms in bedrolls, between campers and tents, past muffled laughter and arguments.

At Sis's step, Gull nickered. She straightened his blanket and talked to him while Murph refilled his water bucket. He seemed calm, but for double safety she fastened his top door shut. Then she and Murph checked the other horses, and found no problems.

Hand in hand, they strolled back to camp. Whether inspired by the starlit night or by the excitement they'd shared, he gave her a good-night kiss. It was too quick to count, because their faces had barely touched when a voice from the dark cheered, "Turn on!" Afterwards, she felt treacherous—pleasantly so—for using Jeff's sleeping bag.

In the chilly dawn light, the campgrounds looked less glamorous. From her bedroll, Sis made out sleeping mounds here and there, scattered boots, kitchen equipment. At her first motion, a head popped up in her own camp. She ignored it, knowing she looked a mess, and as best she could, struggled into her work clothes. Then she dashed for the barn.

That was her first dash. With Gull fed and watered, she next dashed to the rest room, a steamy and slippery place. Then back to camp, where the mothers decided breakfast would be in the 4-H tent.

They ate amid green and white decorations, to a chorus of bleats, squeals, bawling, and cackles. It was a great breakfast—for most people. Sis's stomach reminded her she had the first class this morning, Open Jumpers.

"I'll see you guys after my class," she told the children. "I'll help all of you all day, only let me first get through this class. Uh, alone. Now I'm going to gallop Gull on the track."

"Won't Gull be in the stake, too?" somebody asked.

"Lee wouldn't risk it," Sis admitted. "We had to make entries for here right after Windy Hill, and you remember Gull's performance there."

"Yeah, rotten," said Bobby Nelson.

"Smart-mouth," Murph snapped at him.

A little later, Sis was obliged to accept Bud's offer to watch Gull while she changed. Gull had been spooked when a Future Farmer of America chased a pig past the stall. He shouldn't be left alone. Murph, too, had offered his help, but he was less experienced, and scarcely knew Gull.

Too soon, it seemed, the loudspeaker came on. "Testing—one, two, three. Can you hear me, Ed? This is a heck of a—ouch, I better shut her off.'' But shortly the dreaded call followed, ''Open Jumpers, ten minutes.'' And then, surely in less than ten minutes, ''Open Jumpers to the ring.''

The riders gathered from various barns, about a dozen in all, to stand at the ring gate, some restive, some calm. They gazed in at a carpet of tanbark still smooth, and at brightly painted jumps. Judge and steward were conferring in there, and the ring crew waited to pick up fallen fences—or riders. No, the ambulance man would do that. His long gray car was parked at a discreet distance, under a pine tree.

''Ladies and gentlemen, our National Anthem.''

This opening always tingled the spine, Sis thought. Here the recorded music was a bit scratchy. But nothing could spoil the backdrop, with its dry mountain smell. When the song ended, a meadowlark shot up from the infield with music, this time faultless.

Judges and officials were introduced; the ring gate swung open; the first horse was called. Sis waited to go fourth, a good spot. She studied the course and planned just how to take it: nine fences, in a figure eight. The hardest for Gull, because of his size, would be the in-and-out, to be jumped twice. It was tight, so he'd have to be well-collected to put in a short enough stride between the two parts. Otherwise, there was nothing too tough, though the angles were sharp. Success would depend on how they took those angles, and on his attitude.

So far his attitude was good. In spite of the crowds

and noise, he stood quietly between other horses. He'd raised his head, and turned it a little to follow the rider in the ring, as if he were keeping score. He breathed evenly, and the early heat hadn't dampened his neck.

But Sis felt the heat through her hunt cap, and on her back where the sun beat. She hoped her hands would stay dry, so the reins wouldn't slip if Gull pulled.

"Six faults," the announcer said as the first rider left the ring. Then, "Number ninety, Apache, owned and ridden by Karl Kramer."

Apache's round was short. Three refusals at the in-and-out eliminated him. Poor horse; Sis hated to think how he'd be punished.

So don't think, she told herself, and don't worry. We're going to be lucky. She knew it, because Gull felt just right. There was nothing in there he couldn't jump clean, as long as he wasn't keyed up. And he wasn't. It struck her that she wasn't, either. She thought, this is exactly what I want to do. And I know how to do it. I don't have to depend on luck.

The third rider was the professional who'd ridden so well to win at Windy Hill. She rode just as well now, but a different horse. It was a wild thing that flung itself at its fences, and threatened to take both parts of the in-and-out together. In spite of that, she scored only two faults. She left the ring shaking her head, but the audience applauded her warmly.

Sis felt only a brief flutter at the next call. "Number twelve, Sea Gull. Owned by the Tanbark Ranch, ridden by Sis Reynolds.''

When Gull strode into the ring, his appearance brought scattered applause, quickly hushed.

Just as she'd planned, Sis circled slowly to allow him a better look at the course. He was so relaxed that she had to drive him into a canter for the first fence, a brush. His pace stayed right for the second, the in-and-out, maybe because it faced him before he could speed up. Pop, stride, pop, and they were over it, clean. Change leads now, turn left, sharper, and here's the panel. Let him go. Hey, good, no faults yet! No rap on wood. No sound but muffled hoofbeats and steady blowing. Wind stings the eyes and blurs the wall of faces swinging by. Muscles of horse and rider work together.

Crossed bars next, and circle left or—where? For a ghastly instant Sis was lost. But the next fence—*now*—was the post and rails. Off course or not, Gull cleared it—didn't he? Or was that a tick, or was it flying tanbark? Wow, we've done the sixth fence okay! But look out, we're headed toward the gate—now's when he'll pull. He's starting to! So take back, collect him for the in-and-out once more.

With legs, hands, voice, Sis lifted Gull, steadied him one stride, lifted again. Clean! Somebody yelled "You got it made!" But not yet. A squeeze, more rein, a huge leap to soar over white picket teeth. We're done? *We're done!*

Applause burst out, and cheers from the Tanbark kids. Through the noise, the loudspeaker gave Gull's score, "One half fault." So that *had* been a tick at the post and rails.

Outside the gate, Sis slid off, trying not to smile too widely. Friends surrounded her, but she saw only Gull, her dear great horse. From a cloud, she heard their words.

"You were super!" "Nice goin', Freckles!" "Lee should have been here." "It was perfect."

"No, not perfect," she said. "Half a fault. Someone'll beat us, or we'll have to jump off." She tugged up her hunt cap for air.

"I told you we'd be lucky." It was Bud, and he winked.

"I hope you didn't bet me to win," she said.

"No, to place. You're bound to. If it was me, I'd make ol' Lee share the check."

Sis led Gull aside where she could hear the loudspeaker.

The next ten minutes were agony. As the last horse finished, applause broke out—too much of it. He must have gone clean. She strained to hear the score.

The announcer gave it. "One fault."

No jump off!

The winners were called in for awards, and Sis heard the thrilling words, "First, Number Twelve, Sea Gull, owned by the Tanbark Ranch, ridden by Sis Reynolds."

EIGHT

Sis HAD TO get up as early as usual the next morning, since it was Manuel's Monday off. But getting up wasn't too bad because she could think about yesterday.

It had been almost midnight when the Tanbark bunch got back, after a good show for most of the horses, and a great one for Gull. Too bad he wasn't entered in the stake, they'd all said to Lee.

Lee was waiting up for them, Burper with him. He'd helped unload horses and tack, and sent tired people home. Then he'd talked a while with Sis, and finally left too, and she'd looked in on Gull. He was asleep. "Good night, my horse," she'd said softly, and at last had stumbled off to her cabin.

Now, as she dressed, she thought that at least Manuel would have done his yesterday's work thoroughly. He always made sure there were no leftover jobs for her and Bud. She was eager to see Fury; also Laurie, for Laurie's vacation was due to start.

Down at the Wagon she found the atmosphere stormy. Lee looked his sternest, Laurie defiant.

"Is Fury—?" Sis began timidly.

Lee shook his head, his attention still on Laurie. Then he said, "Fury's doing okay. But he's not used to being shut in. I'll graze him a few minutes today."

"I could do it," Sis offered.

"No, I'll find time," Lee said. "You might let him move too much. Remember it's still six days before his stitches come out."

While Sis ate her breakfast, the other two concluded their argument with a bargain: Laurie was to find another job unless she could give up smoking. She had two weeks' vacation in which to decide.

"Of all the darn nerve!" she fumed when Lee had left. "He figures this is Russia, and he's the king."

Sis didn't think Russia had a king, but that wasn't important. She spent a few minutes reasoning with Laurie, mainly on the basis of friendship. "I'd miss you like crazy if you left for good," she said.

"And I'd miss you, kid," Laurie told her.

"What does Ernie say?"

Laurie's full lips pouted, but she admitted, "He says to quit smoking."

Sis felt she might as well change the subject. "Is your replacement coming tomorrow?"

"Yeah, some old chum of Lee's. Lee has to go fetch him clear from the Delta."

"And he'll sleep in your place?"

"No way. In Lee's office. Say—" Laurie's smile returned. "I heard you were the star yesterday." She never could stay mad long.

The rest of the day, Sis basked in the congratulations of other friends. But next morning, the ranch seemed sad without Laurie, and without Lee, who had gone to fetch his new help. Manuel too for some reason appeared depressed, or troubled, and Sis realized he'd looked that way for a number of days. It might even have been weeks. Now that they could communicate better, she would have to find out what was worrying him.

Meanwhile, while working, she cheered herself by thinking about her date with Jeff tonight. They were to see a movie on TV at his home.

It was good to get away from the ranch for a change, she felt this evening as she sat on the Ashbys' deck enjoying the view and Mrs. Ashby's casserole. For more change, she wore her peasant dress, with the heart-shaped earrings that were supposed to match the gold flecks in her eyes. From Jeff's expression, she concluded that brown hair and eyes weren't exactly repulsive.

The movie was one she'd been wanting to see for years, *National Velvet*. Since it wouldn't start until eight, there was time for talk, more comfortable in a way because Mrs. Ashby was out, playing bridge.

Sis decided that one of the best things about Jeff was his being uncomplicated. On impulse, she tried to tell him so. "After some of the characters at the ranch, it's great to be with someone who's just—well, cheerful. Simple. Nice."

Jeff laughed. "You make me sound half-witted."

"I didn't mean that, and you know it!" Sis gazed off at the city lights. "It's just that people do wrong things, and I always seem to get so upset by them. For instance, certain people cheat in the shows. I can tell they think I'm dumb because I don't."

"So, forget 'em."

"I can't," she said, and thought she was the one who sounded half-witted.

"Want to tell me more?"

She told him about Laurie and her smoking, and finally, to her own surprise, about her dad and his real estate deal.

Talk of one parent led to talk of another, and Jeff spoke of his mother.

"I can't really discuss your dad," he said, "not knowing all the circumstances. But I'll advise *you*: don't try to change the whole world." The light was bright enough to show concern on his face.

"What do you mean?" Sis asked.

"I mean, if you can help people, that's fine. *If*. But you have your life to lead, and they have theirs. Don't knock yourself out trying to make them over. Not many *can* be made over, anyway. I don't mean to depress you, but you may as well realize there'll always be people who'll do what you call wrong things."

"I guess that's true," Sis answered. But she wasn't depressed. On the contrary, a warm sensation filled her. Jeff was the only person to whom she'd confided her dad's story since coming West. What a relief to talk! And how neat that they could act like friends, putting aside for the moment the boy-girl business. She wouldn't have thought it possible. Just the opposite, it added something exciting to their relationship. Maybe maturity was the word.

Soon, settled before the TV, they watched the picture, and for two glorious hours Sis *was* National Velvet.

When Jeff drove her home and parked below her cabin, he left the motor running. Well, all right. She wasn't going to *ask* for his kiss and make a fool of herself. She waited a moment while an owl spoke in the woods. "Hoo hoo. *Hoo hoo*." Another answered, deep and solemn. Then she said, keeping her tone light, "You want me to come back in a year, right?"

Close to her, Jeff chuckled. He didn't touch her, but asked, "Did I say that? How long ago?"

"Almost two months."

"Then come back in ten months."

"It's a date." And Sis left him. She was resigned to playing it his way—temporarily.

But maybe temporarily wasn't going to last long. Inside her cabin, she stood in the dark, listening. Jeff hadn't left—so what was he doing? Would he turn off his motor, and would his footsteps come to her door?

He'd knock, or just walk in, and—

She stopped breathing to hear better. Small sounds of the outdoors intruded. Then the car door slammed. She exhaled. Jeff was leaving.

She switched on her light and said aloud, "Okay, Jeff Ashby, you're taking a chance I'll change my mind. Ten months is a long time."

But the weeks seemed to rush by, so that the middle of August arrived much too soon. The woods were in a dark green shadow, the hills brown, the creek only a gurgle. Sunburned kids wore stark white lips and noses under zinc oxide. Mothers relaxed their discipline. Everyone wished summer would last forever.

"Nothing terrible's happened lately," Sis wrote her sisters one evening. "The barn boys are behaving, though there's always some mystery with them. I mean, at every show Bud bets for or against us, and wins. It's spooky how he figures right each time.

"Manuel won't go off the place alone, although his English is much better. So is my Spanish, which I've been sweating over in a grammar of Jeff's. Besides his wages, now he gets paid by Mrs. McCauley, one of our grandmas, for yard work. Still he looks worried, and once or twice he tried to tell me something, and then veered off as if he was afraid.

"Doctor Nesbit took out Fury's stitches, and his lovely foretop is growing bushy again. Lee's in a good mood, nobody knows why. Mrs. Ashby took some of us shopping in San Francisco. I spent most of my money in a neat saddle store on grooming tools for Gull. Mrs. Ashby pointed out the Hall of Sports that even you guys must have heard about. It'll house nearly a thousand horses next month for the National, and Jeff's promised we'd go see it as our last date before I leave for home. And Laurie and Ernie got back today, and now I have to go help her unpack, so I'll finish this later.''

Laurie was prowling the Wagon with a frown.

"Shorty sure left things clean for you," Sis remarked.

"Hmm." Laurie sniffed. "Trying to steal my job. Or to give Lee ideas, like keeping this dump old-maid neat.''

Sis was about to ask if Laurie'd quit smoking when Lee walked in. He too looked extra neat in a suit, which changed his image. She wondered if this was due to Shorty's influence, and smiled at the thought.

Lee must have misread her smile, for he asked us if nervous, "Don't I look all right?''

"You look fine," she said.

"Classy," Laurie added. Then she asked, "You wanted something?''

Lee's gray eyes roamed the room, until he said almost sheepishly, "I forget.''

The girls looked at each other, then at him.

"You're going out?" Sis asked.

"Well, yes.''

"Dating?" Laurie suggested. This was incredible!

"I figure," Lee answered, "you could call it that. I'm taking Bitsie out."

Two voices echoed, "Bitsie?"

At the door he mumbled, "Doctor Nesbit," and disappeared.

The girls collapsed in each other's arms. Somehow the picture of Lee dating was too much. Together they repeated "Bitsie!" until tears of mirth weakened them.

"So that's what's been goin' on!" Laurie cried, wiping her eyes.

"And that's why he's been so mellow," said Sis.

Lee continued to be mellow and, Sis reflected, so did Gull—at least with her. Around strangers, he still cocked an ear or rolled an eye, and the muffled snorts said, "I don't quite trust you." But with her, he'd become so responsive that they no longer argued, and she could concentrate on perfecting his jumping, or their jumping together. During the summer, she'd shortened his stride, improved his mouth, and in general relaxed him. Naturally, Lee was aware of these changes. So must the horse show crowd be, including Karl Kramer. Sis could only hope to make Gull so valuable to Lee that Lee wouldn't sell him.

At rare intervals Gull was still flighty. Yet at recent shows his score had been excellent, sometimes super. So why not at all shows? Sis gave this a lot of thought, and tried to recall everything her coach had taught her back home.

Not being a jump rider himself, Lee couldn't solve

the problem. But he agreed that Sis should call her old coach for advice.

On the phone, she answered dozens of questions: on just how Gull misbehaved, and in what circumstances; what bit she was using; how she cued and rated him; how she communicated through hands, legs, and voice; whether she'd developed any bad habits. Her coach asked about Gull's feed, schooling, weight, shoeing, work schedule, and health. Had he had his shots? Teeth floated? Wormed?

Finally, he said, "It seems I can't help you, Sis, without seeing you jump this horse. Do you know anyone who'd take movies of you?"

Sis had to say no.

"Stills, then?"

"Yes."

"All right, send them along, and I'll comment by mail. Will you be showing at National, in the Hall of Sports?"

Sis smiled. "Gosh, no. We don't have that good a stable."

Each day, school's opening date crept closer with the first hints of fall. The weather didn't seem to have changed, yet sunlight was a trace less golden, twilight came a trace earlier. Sis couldn't bear to think of leaving. Already she had plans for Christmas vacation.

"I'll hitchhike back if I have to," she told Jeff.

"Don't even think of doing that," he said very soberly.

He'd come to take pictures of her jumping. Then they'd double date with Laurie and Ernie, a date that would include finishing the treehouse. Jeff wasn't her only date. She'd gone out twice with Murph. But both times were disappointing. Murph wasn't exciting. Kind of fun—but only kind of.

By the time Jeff arrived, hurrying from work, Lee and the boys had set up four fences outside the ring where the light was good. Gull was bathed and saddled, Sis ready in clean breeches and shirt, shined boots and brushed hunt cap. She'd really worked over Gull's tack, too, so her coach wouldn't think she'd grown sloppy.

With newly acquired patience, Gull stood for her to mount. Together they looked over the jumps, placed roughly in a circle as space allowed.

"Just what would your coach want to see?" Jeff asked her.

"Most likely fences of different heights," she said, "and maybe a few turns and stops."

Within minutes she was on her first round, trying hard to make it look polished. She succeeded so well that when she'd pulled up, Jeff said, "How's a man going to criticize that performance?" But she suspected the pictures would show some faults to a professional eye.

Lee didn't say anything; even now his mind might be on Bitsie. Then Sis saw his expression, keen as ever, and heard his smug words, "Looks like I wasn't

108

wrong.'' Whatever that meant.

On the sidelines Bud prompted, ''Raise 'em up?''

''Six inches—and *I*'ll measure,'' Lee answered, showing his measuring stick.

Jeff changed his position for the best shot at Gull over the post and rails, now widened as well as heightened.

Sis took a deep seat and came at it in a strong gallop. Just where she'd calculated, she tightened her legs, cued Gull with a cluck, and gave him the rein he needed. He was over with a leap that landed him well beyond. She took back to steady him, then again increased his pace facing the brush. Lee had laid a pole on top of it, and at her signal Gull cleared it too as if it were on fire.

A tight turn, and they were headed for what Sis called ''the Lee special.'' This was a row of the ranch's metal trash cans on crates. Their height wasn't over four ten, but gave the illusion of being more, perhaps because of the flashing sunlight on them.

As Gull neared them, his ears pricked, and for a second his stride faltered, but Sis drove him on. He responded with a bound that could have left her behind if she hadn't been prepared. Airborne, she heard the click of Jeff's camera, and Manuel's *''Dios!''*

The photography went on until Jeff was confident that he had a number of good pictures. Then Sis jumped down and started to lead Gull off with the praise he deserved. Passing Lee, she caught his words, ''Yessir, I was right.''

She couldn't resist asking, "About what?"

"Keep walking," was the answer.

But a few minutes later, he joined her where she was rubbing down Gull, cross-tied in his aisle.

"When does school start?"

His question surprised her, but she didn't stop grooming to answer, "Just after Labor Day."

The subject seemed closed, because he said next, "Use your hoof pick." But when she straightened after some moments, he asked, "So you'll still be free Labor Day weekend?"

"Yes."

Conversationally, he went on, "That's the weekend of the Hall of Sports Show."

"I know." He was going to invite her to see some of it, a bonus before she left. They might double date with Jeff and Bitsie. Swell.

She unsnapped Gull's cross tie and led him into his stall. After a drink, he walked over to his feed pan and rattled it, a call for supper. She stepped from the stall, but Lee was talking.

"I believe Gull could handle those courses as well as any horse."

She paused. "What courses?"

"In the Hall of Sports."

She felt herself flush, tried to swallow, and managed to blurt, "Were you—you weren't—thinking of showing him there?"

Lee nodded. Both stared at Gull. Then Sis said in a

dead tone, ''The entries must be closed.''

''Yup,'' said Lee.

''And a National show like that, they won't take post entries?''

''Right.'' A spark lit his eyes, as if this were humorous, as if he enjoyed torturing her.

''Post entries wouldn't help,'' he said.

Baffled, bitter, desperate with hope, she gazed at him.

''Because,'' he concluded, ''Gull's already entered.''

NINE

It SEEMED TO Sis that suddenly she was the most important person on the ranch—or at least someone special. Two days had passed since Lee's amazing news, and already everybody knew that Gull was entered at the Hall of Sports, and that Sis would ride him.

While she worked as usual, her mood was anything but usual. It teetered from high, when she pictured impossible victories, to lower than low when she saw herself falling, going off course, or, worst of all, wrecking Gull in a gory crash. Thoughts of the big entry fee Lee had paid, of the trainers she'd ride against, of how green she was still—all this kept her in turmoil that outweighed her elation.

As the days passed, other people met her attitude in characteristic ways.

Laurie advised, with a shrug of plump shoulders, "If you don't want to ride in the big one, don't do it."

"But I'm dying to," Sis said miserably.

Jeff told her she'd enjoy every minute in "the Hall." He'd had a raise, so was annoyingly cheerful himself.

Bud said, "Keep away from me, grouch," and Sis flared, "With pleasure."

Mrs. Ashby praised her for her nerve in wanting to jump enormous fences. "Myself, I'd die of fright," she said, which struck Sis as a sensible outlook.

Of course the kids were thrilled by the news. But they had their own interests, and their excitement subsided, temporarily. Sis knew it would accelerate again when the fateful day neared, in only two weeks.

Manuel didn't seem to notice any change in her, but she noticed increasing depression in him.

Looking uneasy, he followed her one morning into Gull's stall. "Señorita," he said, "there is a thing I tell you."

"A thing?"

He nodded, glanced about, then muttered, "A bad thing."

For a moment Gull needed her attention. When she turned back, Manuel had gone, as furtively as a shadow. She guessed why, seeing Lee in his place. Well, she would find Manuel later. But that day she was so much absorbed by her own affairs that she forgot him.

If Lee noticed her moodiness, he wasn't about to humor her. This was understandable. After all, his money and his horse were involved. He wouldn't want a jockey with finicky moods. He became if anything more businesslike, with instructions about a tighter schedule for Gull.

"Not more schooling," he said. "But grain him, and add a portion of those vitamin pellets or powders, Drive or Go-Boy. I'll buy the best. He's got to feel high to clear those high fences."

Sis shuddered. With Lee, she stood at Gull's stall door, looking in.

"He has to be fit—and you too," Lee went on. "So get up earlier and gallop him in the ring every morning, and get in some hill work too. That'll leg you up as well. No rag doll can handle a thirteen hundred pound thoroughbred."

Sis steadied her voice to ask, "Which fences shall I practice?"

"I'll tell you which and when," Lee said. And he asked abruptly, "How much do you weigh?"

"About a hundred and twenty."

"Don't lose any," he ordered. "You'll need every ounce." It sounded ominous.

While another week passed, Sis knew she was losing weight in spite of Lee's orders. Meanwhile, Gull was becoming a powerhouse of muscle, explosive with good health. When he pranced, his dapples seemed to bounce with a life of their own. Yet his manners had improved to a satisfying extent. So had her horsemanship, Sis realized. Her coach had said so too in his answering letter. She supposed her loss of weight was due partly to hours of added riding, partly because her appetite had dwindled. Laurie noticed that, but couldn't help.

Strangely, help came from Bitsie, a week before the show.

The girls had grown used to seeing her on visits that they suspected weren't all strictly necessary. From referring to her in private as ''Bitsie,'' it seemed natural to call her that to her face. In her white coveralls, she appeared fresh even after dirty jobs, and pleasant, though with something of Lee's bluntness. The fact that Lee no longer used any other vet proved that he admired Bitsie's work. He wouldn't have let her touch a horse just because he admired her as a woman. Elsewhere, too, her reputation must be tops, for she'd been selected one of three vets to serve the long weekend at the Hall.

Bitsie wasn't in work clothes the evening she stepped from her pickup in front of the Wagon. She looked very feminine in a short yellow dress. To Sis who joined her, she said, ''I'll wait for Lee. Probably he's changing in his office.''

Through with her day's work, Sis strolled to the pasture gate with Bitsie, who wanted a look at Fury. Their voices brought him slithering down the hill on his matchstick legs, with snatches of whinnies as high pitched as Melissa's voice.

''I hardly thought he'd make it, a few weeks ago,'' Bitsie said. ''Now he has more pep than you.''

''Yes, I'm a mess,'' Sis answered, too depressed to

care. She shoved her hands with their bitten nails into her pockets.

Bitsie began to talk, not unkindly, but firmly, about Sis's attitude toward riding in the Hall. What she said made Sis first angry, then ashamed.

The gist of Bitsie's talk was that Sis was selfish in giving way to her moods; that she was unfair to Lee, to Gull, and to herself. That she must either tell Lee to find another rider— "There *are* others, you know, good ones, who'd give anything to ride in the Hall"—or Sis must pull herself together and behave like an adult responsible for a job.

Bitsie might have said more, but Lee and Burper interrupted. She ended, with a smile for Sis, "If you want to talk this over, call me in the morning. Before seven."

But Sis had seen the light at the end of the tunnel. "We can skip that," she answered. "What you said is all true. And—well, thank you."

Lee took Bitsie's arm and told her, "You might not feel so sharp before seven A.M. tomorrow. We'll be out late. And what's to talk about anyway?"

"Girl stuff, no boys allowed," said Bitsie with an impudent grin.

He glanced at his watch. "Come on, then, girl," and he walked her off.

Burper burped, and Sis picked him up. Deep in thought, she carried him to the Wagon. The light she saw mentally wasn't dazzling—yet, but it was an exciting spark. She was still thoughtful over supper.

"You look almost human," Laurie remarked.

"I've decided to enjoy life."

"About time."

At her bedtime check on Gull, Sis laughed aloud when he greeted her. Even his voice was changing, to a deeper, stronger tone. So he must have sounded, and looked, as a stallion. Magnificent.

In her cabin she prepared for reading and a good night's sleep. It would be the first in weeks, for sleep had been restless lately, although the treehouse, now completed, made a fine bedroom. How many people, she wondered, could see stars through branches from their bedroll, hear a stream below them, smell its moist banks, and listen to owls call back and forth in the black woods. . . .

She was awakened only an hour or so later, it seemed, by something falling on her head. Groping, she removed a twig. "Hey, up there, quit it, Whisk," she mumbled. It was cozy, though, to think of him in his twiggy bed high above hers. How cute, a squirrel in bed!

She turned over, and then, for the third time, she saw it—a glow through the skylight of Lee's storeroom. This third time was too much. It couldn't be accidental. Besides, the light wasn't there when she'd gone to bed, so Lee hadn't left it on.

Frightened, she jerked on her robe over pajamas and hurried barefoot down toward Gull's barn. She scarcely felt the rough footing, only the banging of her heart.

Her steps into the barn were so stealthy that even Gull didn't hear them. But any second he'd sense her presence and reveal it. On toptoe, hardly breathing, she approached the storeroom door. Like the last time, it was open a crack. Inside, somebody moved. She half expected it to be Bud.

One more step, at which Gull discovered her, and rumbled deep in his throat.

A voice cursed behind the open door. Bud's voice? Sis wasn't sure.

But Gull sensed trouble since she hadn't answered him. He circled his stall noisily, then began to paw.

A mutter came from the storeroom. The door was pushed wider and Bud stepped into the aisle.

Sis saw a stack of cartons in the room, and a syringe, bottles, and glass vials on the floor. The shaft of light pinned her in full view.

Bud gaped at her from the threshold. Then he reached for the doorknob.

"Don't close it!" she cried. The thought of being alone with him in the dark aisle terrified her. "I mean, it's too late," she blurted. She'd seen what surely must be drug supplies, and he knew she'd seen them.

Still, he tried a bluff. "Look what I found!"

She stepped into the storeroom. After a glance at the items on the floor and at Bud's face, she said, "There's no use lying, Bud. All that stuff—it's yours, isn't it?" His manner, as well as the evidence, convinced her that it was.

He scooped everything into an open carton, pushed

the carton into place, and piled on it other cartons, dusty and evidently empty. That done, he faced her, and before her eyes he seemed to deflate. He was pale, his glance shifty. His whole person admitted guilt.

It struck her that she needn't be scared, because *he* was scared. "Turn out the light and lock up and let's get out of here," she said. "Lee and Bitsie'll be coming back." She tightened her robe about her.

"Not yet. They went to Frisco. I heard 'em talk." Bud's tone was plain misery. "What—what're you gonna do?"

Sis asked herself the same question as they walked from the barn. There was only one answer, and it took nerve to give it. "I'll have to tell Lee what I saw."

To her horror, Bud broke out crying, great rasping sobs that would have been pitiful from a child. From him, they were shocking. They shook him so that he couldn't walk on.

Beside him, Sis stood in the starlit road, panicked by the whole scene. What if Lee returned and found her here in pajamas? What if Laurie for some reason came out, or Manuel came looking for Bud? And what about Bud? Alone with her, he might do something crazy.

Sis grasped his arm and tugged. Minutes later they reached the haystack and sat on a fallen bale.

Bud acted relieved to admit everything. Yes, he'd picked the storeroom lock; that was easy. Yes, the drugs were his, but not stolen; he'd been buying them from a friend at the Albany racetrack. They weren't for humans, only animals.

"*Only* animals!" Sis flared. Then she remembered Manuel. What was his share in all this?

"He knows about it," Bud said, "but he don't want no part in it. He told me he'd report it to Lee, only he don't have the nerve. See, I know that Manuel's an illegal alien. If the cops find this out, they'll deport him. So—" Bud snickered, "Manuel don't dare talk."

But Manuel would have talked—to her, Sis thought, and guilt assailed her. She should have made time, given him a chance.

She hated the sound of Bud's snuffling, and sight of his damp face. Moving away from him on the hay bale, she made herself ask, "What were you doing with those drugs in the storeroom?"

Hay crackled as Bud shifted. After a pause he answered, "Sometimes I use 'em on horses."

"Horses! What for?"

Silence.

"*Our* horses? Why?"

More silence. Then, "Only one horse," Bud mumbled.

Now with dreadful foreboding Sis forced out the words, "Which one?"

Bud's reply was so low that she didn't hear it. Loudly now, she repeated, "*Which one*?"

This time, she caught the answer.

A frightening thing happened to her. Out of control, her lips started to tremble. This had never occurred before because she'd never before felt such outrage. She turned from Bud so that she wouldn't hit him, and plunged her clenched fists into the pockets of her robe.

Behind her, Bud said, "It don't hurt him. Just the opposite, when he's kinda sedated, he likes to jump. You'd of known that, bein' on him at the shows where he went good, only you never knew why he went good."

Sis was too stunned, too appalled, to answer. But when she could control herself she asked, "That's why you always won your bets on him—because you'd either doped him or not, so you knew how he'd act?"

"Sure." Bud sounded smug.

"You're repulsive!" she burst out.

"Hey, wait a minute!" Hurt, was he? He deserved to be killed.

"All my work," Sis raged, "my hopes for Gull, his improvement, our teaming together, and Lee's plans—all—oh, I can't take it!" Sudden tears gushed down her face, and she slapped them away.

The nightmare continued, and now Sis didn't care if Lee and Bitsie turned up. She cared only about what Bud had done to Gull. "You've made him an addict!" she cried.

"Aw, knock it off. I've made him willing to jump and to win. Look at it that way. Can't you see him sailin' over those fences in the Hall? He could do it easy. He's an athlete. But he won't do it if he's nervous or fighting. Give him a break."

Bud took a breath and continued firmly. "You don't

understand how the stuff works. It gives a horse courage, like it steadies him. Then when you decrease it, he still behaves himself, because by now he's forgot his old bad ways. What it does, it makes life easier for him.''

As Sis didn't answer, he went on, ''You'll cash in too, betting as well as winning, if you'll agree to—all right, all right, forget it.'' He was backing away from her retort.

The scene took a new turn when he said, ''If you get me kicked out, what'll happen to Manuel? He'd be lost without me.''

It was true in a way, Sis thought. Bud wasn't good for Manuel, yet without him Manuel might go all the way downhill fast.

As she hesitated, Bud pressed his advantage, telling her how he had already bet every cent he and Manuel could raise on Gull's winning a class at the Hall. Manuel—bullied by Bud, Sis guessed—had sold his radio and his half share of a bicycle, which had taken him months to accumulate. They'd borrowed, and were paying interest on the loans. Both had been working nights, Bud with Ernie, Manuel for Mrs. McCauley.

''It'd wreck Manuel to lose everything,'' Bud finished. ''And he'd maybe think I been fooling him, because I just about promised Gull can win.''

''But what do you tell him, about your bets and so on?'' Sis asked.

''Just that I know horses. And I know what your

competition will be at the Hall. I been doin' some sleuthing.''

"If you know horses, you should know better than to promise a horse can win.''

Gull could still win without drugs, Sis thought. But in the circumstances, she wasn't certain. It would depend, she supposed, on how much he'd been getting, and—oh, what a ghastly mess. And the risk for Lee! As Gull's owner, he'd be fined and set down if Gull were tested and found drugged. She closed her eyes and shook her head, trying to think.

Bud cut short her effort, his tone so reasonable that she had to listen. "Let me do it one more time. Just this once at the Hall, to help all of us. Then you can tell Lee, because I'll be gone. You guys'll take care of Manuel, or he can go with me; and Gull won't be none the worse. Heck, he's never had enough to miss it, not enough to hurt a baby.''

A small breeze stirred. Sis wondered what time it was, and how long she dared stay. Sound of a car on the ranch road was her answer. She jumped up with a smothered "They're back!''

"They won't see us,'' Bud said, he too on his feet. "Come on, behind the hay.''

Motionless in the darker dark back of the haystack, Sis listened to Lee's pickup drive in, stop, then follow Bitsie out. Disgust filled her for what she was doing— hiding, barefoot, not even dressed, alongside this creep who'd tricked her, Lee, and their horse. Now he was asking her to help "make life easier" for Gull at the Hall. . . . Well, she hadn't said yes—or no.

Before she slept that night, she thought for a long time of the phrase about making life easier for Gull.

TEN

NEXT MORNING ON her way to Gull's early workout, Sis knew that her answer to helping Bud must be no. She was ashamed that she'd considered anything else even for a minute. She must have been insane last night. Bud, and the shock, and the darkness, had unnerved her. But no more of that. She would not only tell him no, she'd also tell Lee the whole story. She owed Lee that. Then they'd be rid of Bud, and she'd feel honest again. Lee would know what was best for Manuel.

"But one good thing," she said to Gull in his barn, speaking thoughtfully, "this business has made me realize how tempting it can be to cheat." For the first time, she understood a little of what her dad had gone through. She wasn't angry at him any more, only sorry that he'd pull a shabby deal.

"Hey, I forgot," she told Gull, "this is Grandma Day. We'll do our hill work with them. Ring work now. Jumps, Lee said, and he'll coach us."

Her spirits were so lifted by relief at her decision that they seemed to lift both her and Gull over the fences. Their approaches, timing, landings, their form, all were good. Gull made only one mistake, taking off too soon at the brush because she'd cued him too soon. It seemed he could do perfectly well without drugs.

When Lee was satisfied, he said, "Not bad."

Sis graded herself B+. Her coach would have been pleased. He'd been too pleased by her photos to be of real help.

Walking out, she said to Lee, "I envy Bitsie. She'll get to spend that whole long weekend at the Hall!"

"Working hard," said Lee drily.

"Will she commute?"

"No, she'll stay over there at the motel where most of the horse crowd stays."

Sis wondered if she should talk to Lee privately now. It seemed only fair, for some reason, to tackle Bud first much as she hated him—but not yet.

During breakfast with Laurie, she was aware that she dreaded the talk with Bud. Maybe she should postpone it. . . . But shortly he discovered her, saddling for the grandmas. She was at one end of the tie-stall row, working toward Manuel at the other.

Between a horse's shoulder and the partition, Bud sidled up to her. He asked, low, "You made up your mind about doing it at the Hall?"

She nodded. "I made up my mind that I won't do it."

His mouth tightened. His eyes slitted down at her.

"So you won't play it my way?"

"No." There was no use explaining. Most likely he'd expected this answer anyway.

His glance traveled the length of the tie-stall row. Seeing only Manuel, he stepped forward, crowding Sis against the manger.

She looked down at his hand that had grabbed her wrist, and saw its coarse knuckles, and smelled his dirty breath. But she returned his stare, forcing herself with every nerve.

Finally, he flung down her hand and grunted, "You'll be sorry, you and that nag. I'll make sure of that."

She couldn't think of an answer. If only he'd *go*!

But, starting to back out, he threatened, "I'm tellin' you, you better smarten up and change your mind." His furtive eyes checked again that they were alone. Then he leaned forward and asked on a lower tone, "You wouldn't want Gull to have an accident, would you?"

Sis felt the manger's edge hard against her back. It was only after he'd gone that she realized her knees were trembling.

She left the rest of the saddling to Manuel, which must have puzzled him. Still shaky, she ran to Gull's stall. He was all right—but she'd worry about him unless they were together. Even so, she'd worry until Lee knew about Bud and his threats. Yet Lee's knowing might trigger Bud's revenge. Whatever she did could be wrong.

Now the grandmas' arrival dismayed her. There'd be no chance to talk with Lee until later. She had to saddle Gull.

Soon she was following the twittering group, who this time chose Redwood Trail for their outing. They said nice things to her that she didn't deserve, for she was untidy and inattentive. It didn't help that Lee was cool toward her. He knew she'd left half her work to Manuel. Gull clearly sensed her worry, for he acted subdued. No prancing on the redwood needles, but a solemn walk under the great trees. No shying at the creek, which now was low, and slid by quietly. The woods' hush seemed to foreshadow disaster.

When they stopped to rest, it was in a redwood grove whose giants made midgets of humans and horses.

"Like a cathedral," Mrs. Olsen said. "I feel we should whisper." And another grandma added, "Let's absorb the beauty and fragrance, to recall, girls."

Lee rode a few lengths away to water his mare in a dark pool. At that, Sis jumped down and joined him, and blurted, "Can I talk to you a minute? I've got to!"

Her expression must have convinced him. "Go ahead, but keep it down," he said with a glance at his charges.

While their two horses drank, Sis told of Bud's drugging, of what he planned to do at the Hall, and how he'd said, "You wouldn't want Gull to have an accident?" The action of three months took hardly three minutes to tell.

Lee's only answer was to call out, "Ready, ladies?" With that, he swung onto his mare, and Sis had to scramble on Gull or be left.

The return trip was a bit fast for the grandmas. Several complained mildly, but Lee played deaf. Sis suspected they were disappointed when, at the barn, Manuel met them without a smile. Lee ordered her to help unsaddle the rent horses, then, on Gull, to teach a private lesson in his place. Nothing about Bud.

The tanbark dust made her head ache. Or maybe it was nerves. The ranch was too quiet. Something must be going on that she couldn't see or hear. That hunch seemed right when Anita Pickett appeared and asked, "Where's Bud?"

"Most likely with Lee," Sis answered, picturing a stormy scene in Lee's office.

After the lesson and through feeding time, quiet persisted. Only a few parents and youngsters wandered about. Nobody fed the horses in pasture, and they lined the fence, waiting with ears pricked and frequent pawing.

Sis hung around the deserted barn, hesitant to leave Gull. She was considering a visit to Laurie when Lee appeared.

"Come to my office," he said. Outside the barn, he saw the horses waiting at the pasture fence and added, "We'll feed 'em later."

Lee's office looked strange to Sis because of the people there—Laurie and Ernie, Manuel, Anita in tears, now Lee and herself, and a large man introduced as Sheriff McGraph.

The sheriff eyed her keenly as he said, "We're trying to locate Bud."

She looked from one face to another, all blank.

"Any idea where he could be?" he asked her.

"Why—no."

"Think carefully. These folks don't know, but it seems you were one of the last to see him, this morning."

Sis turned to Manuel, who shrugged. "He says only *adiós*," Manuel told her. His face was pale, his dark eyes large with fright. She remembered that he'd always feared the law. But evidently he and the others had answered questions satisfactorily, for they were excused.

The sheriff continued to question Sis alone, while evening darkened beyond the open door. When a car drove in, she recognized the sound of Jeff's VW. Of course—they had a date. She'd forgotten.

Free at last, she found Jeff at Gull's stall where he knew she'd turn up. He had news for her, having talked with Lee.

"Lee's going to sleep next to Gull tonight, in the storeroom, just in case Bud takes a notion to prowl. Ernie called his boss and got time off to stay with Laurie. Manuel will get along by himself in the trailer, I guess. And you're coming home with me."

"But—"

"No buts. I'll bring you back early tomorrow."

Sis gave in, but suggested, "Let's at least say good night to Manuel; he must be miserable."

But Manuel appeared resigned, maybe even relieved. He'd borrowed Burper for company, and was looking through some of Sis's old magazines. He said to her shyly, "Is good everybody knows about the drugs. Now I don't have to tell, *verdad*?"

"*Verdad*," Sis agreed.

Leaving Jeff with Manuel, she went to her cabin to pack an overnight bag. Evidently the sheriff had organized a search of the ranch, for she heard strange voices in odd directions, and saw lights, some high on the hills. It was as if monster dragonflies hovered here and there. Creepy. Her wild little neighbors were silent, maybe fearful too. Even Whisk had vanished.

When Jeff came for her, she was relieved to go, knowing Gull wouldn't be alone.

She sat close to Jeff in the little car, glad to hear his voice and once his deep chuckle, to glimpse a flash of sun-bleached hair in the passing lights. They hadn't seen each other alone much lately. Sis realized that she'd missed him, a lot. She wished that she could tell him so. But the more she wished it, the more awkward she felt.

Much later, in the Ashbys' lovely guest room, she thought again of Gull, and some words of Jeff's returned to haunt her. Between the linen sheets she shivered, remembering: "In case Bud takes a notion to prowl tonight.'' *Prowl*, a horrible word. . . . It hinted at stealthy footsteps nearing in the dark, at breathing withheld, at a smell you couldn't identify, vibrations you couldn't explain. . . .

"You've been reading too much," she said to herself. "Go to sleep."

But the curtains stirred at the windows, and sounds of the city intruded.

Next morning at daylight she tiptoed to the kitchen, looking for the telephone.

There she met Mrs. Ashby, also tiptoeing, and the two laughed. Tempting smells of bacon and toast floated about, but the view drew Sis to the window. In the sparkling light, San Francisco's skyline was sharp across the bay, a sensational sight. The Hall wasn't visible. Thought of it sobered her. Opening night, next Friday, was only six days away.

At the stove, Mrs. Ashby said, "Call Jeff, dear, will you? He's the second door down the hall."

First Sis telephoned the ranch. The phone rang unanswered in Lee's office, so she called the Wagon. Ernie answered, complained at being wakened, and said everything was fine.

"How do you know?" Sis asked.

"I'd know if it wasn't," he said, and she had to be satisfied with that.

There was a delightful intimacy in breakfasting with the Ashbys in their sun-flooded kitchen, even though Jeff looked grumpy. He resembled a schoolboy half awake, which made Sis feel mature.

"My son always wakes up in this stunned condition," Mrs. Ashby told her with a smile.

"Better stunned than stoned," Jeff mumbled. He watched suspiciously as Sis refilled his cup, and he asked, "You're so old-fashioned that you'd wait on a man?"

"Only on a zombie," she retorted. "And only so you'll have strength to drive me back to the ranch."

Half an hour later Lee joined them as they were carrying Sis's belongings up to her cabin. He startled her with the words, "Don't unpack."

She waited for more.

It came just as tersely. "You're leaving."

Gosh, I'm fired, she thought, but still couldn't speak.

It was Jeff who asked, "How come?"

Impatiently, Lee explained. "Bud was seen last night at Blanche's, so we figure he's too close for comfort. I've decided to move Gull to the Hall."

"And me too? When? Now? I'm ready!" The words tumbled from Sis.

Lee gave her one of his tight smiles. He handed Jeff a padlock, saying, "Lock this cabin when she's got her stuff out, whatever she'll need, and give Laurie the key. I nailed the window closed." To Sis he said, "You and Gull be ready in a couple of hours. Clean him good, but not a bath. Set out a fresh blanket and leg wraps, and see that his grooming box is all together." Turned away, he paused to add, "Don't forget anything, because you won't be back till after the whole show. I'll make it back and forth, but you'll stay there and take care of Gull."

"Maybe I'll sleep with him—neat!" Sis breathed, at which Jeff snorted.

Twenty minutes later she was packed, the cabin safely secured, Jeff gone. In high gear she ran down with the key and a good-bye hug for Laurie.

To her surprise, she found Murph at work in Gull's barn. He was taking Bud's place, he said; he'd come before and after school. Sis hoped he'd move into the trailer with Manuel. But right now she had time only for Gull.

This being Sunday, children, parents, and other clients were arriving already. Word had spread that Sis and Gull were leaving for the Hall. Everyone wanted to help them get ready. The adults knew the reason for this sudden move; the kids apparently were too excited to wonder. Melissa summed up their feelings: "Sis Reynolds, you're the luckiest Ms. in the whole United States."

"In the universe," Bethie corrected.

Sis had to shut her mind to their chatter while she brushed and curried Gull. Bobby steadied the stool on which she stood to do Gull's mane and foretop. Another youngster cleaned her saddle, another polished her bit and stirrup irons.

Cross-tied in the aisle, Gull looked tremendous.

Plainly, he liked being the center of commotion. He must know by the preparations that he was going to a show. Even now he was listening for the sound of the van outside.

When Sis heard it, she was packing the grooming box, reciting, "Hoof pick, sponge, comb, two brushes, hoof grease, towels, clippers, liniment, shampoo, soap—what else?" she asked the eager faces.

"Lee'll take a broom and pitchfork," somebody said.

A mother suggested "Medications?" Then she added quickly, "Just in case."

"Yes, and scissors, and a hammer, and what else?"

In the background, Manuel spoke softly. "*Sombrero*?"

"*Sombrero*—hat—oh, my hunt cap! I have it. Thanks, Manuel." They heard Lee coming, and made way.

"Zip on his leg wraps," said Lee, "and blanket him. I'll load some feed." Minutes later, "All set?"

Sis glanced around in panic, sure she'd forgotten something—but what?

She led the big horse out, and up the ramp into the van. She'd ride with him. Semidarkness fell with the closing doors.

Above the crunch of tires, the kids shouted, "Good-bye!" "Win everything!" "Good luck!" " 'Bye, Gull!" Lastly, Melissa shrieked, "We're waving, Ms.!"

ELEVEN

"HI, GALS," SIS wrote her sisters, scribbling fast by flashlight. "I tried twice to call you, but phone booths here are always full, and there's not much privacy with a roommate. You see, I'm in a motel, with Doctor Nesbit, this super lady vet. Of course, both of us are here for the Hall show. We came early, which I'll explain when I get home."

Sis shifted her pad and paused to listen. No sounds came from the other bed, only from the street where already cars sped by, their headlights sweeping the window. How anyone could sleep here was amazing. It must be even noisier in the daytime, but Sis's days were spent with Gull. Luckily this motel was within walking distance of the Hall, but those walks in the dark were scary. Mornings, she ran, pretending it was for her health. At night, usually she got a ride from Bitsie or some horseman staying here.

"I've made friends with our stall neighbors," she

wrote. "They're a nice couple from Oregon, with a terrific black jumper. But there aren't many people my age. It's an adult world, mostly professionals, and they're not in it for fun. Everybody has arrived by now, and the pressure's growing every minute. It gets to me, but the worst should be over when you read this."

A truck passed with a rattle and roar that brought a groan from Bitsie, then a whispered, "Awake, Sis?"

"Hours ago," Sis said, and snapped off her flashlight.

"You're nervous."

"Well, opening night's tomorrow, and I'm in it, the first class."

"If you weren't nervous, I'd worry about you," Bitsie said.

"Gull's getting nervous, too," Sis told her. "He hates the crowds, and people trying to pet him, like in a petting zoo. I'm sure he'd like to bite one. And the noise upsets him when he's eating. He'll grab a mouthful and then wheel and drop it. And with lights on all night he's not sleeping well."

Sis heard Bitsie sit up to ask, "You can tell by his bedding in the morning?"

"Yes, it's so churned up the stall's hard to clean."

After a silence Bitsie said, "If he were mine, I'd give him a long rest when this show's over. He's been campaigned steadily all summer, and Lee's pleased with his improvement. A vacation would improve him even more, for next year's circuit."

"Then I'd see him when I come back at Christmas."

Sis noticed neither one mentioned the chance of Gull being sold.

Bitsie was up now, groping toward the light switch. "Why don't you lease him?" she asked. "That way, you could be sure he gets his rest, turned out at the ranch. I'd keep an eye on him for you."

It was an exciting idea. Sis had saved most of her salary, and if Gull won here, she'd get a cut of the purse. He *had* to do well tomorrow night. As Lee said, Gull's first performance would show what he would or could do the rest of the weekend. But at the moment, Sis wasn't sure she'd survive that long.

Her doubts increased with the passing hours, while she tried to hide what the strain was doing to her. She avoided talking because she had no idea what she might say. She failed to recognize people she knew. In the Hall's cafeteria, she forced herself to eat. Only with Gull she felt calmer because he kept her busy. No horse in the Hall was better cared for. Besides, she wanted above all to soothe his tension, not communicate more.

Somehow she got through the day, and Jeff helped her through the evening. He brought her the ranch news, took her to dinner, and made her laugh. She felt he was good for her because he really didn't understand how nervous she was. When he took her back to the motel, Bitsie was just getting back too, with Lee. All four sat on the beds and talked until abruptly exhaustion overcame Sis and she fell asleep fully dressed.

When she woke, the window showed a hint of daylight, and someone was talking in the next room.

"It's Mason, the stockhorse man," Bitsie said. "His mare's on my list of ill and injured."

Sis heard without interest the list of Bitsie's patients. She fumbled into work clothes, with no sensation except that her stomach felt weird. At the door she said, "I'll come back to change before tonight." Then she stepped out into a wall of fog.

Fog engulfed her. It crawled on her skin and into her mouth. It tasted like some choking cold soup. It muffled sounds and blurred lights along the avenue. Lucky, she thought, that she couldn't get lost. But she didn't dare run for fear of smashing into somebody, both their steps soundless. The thought struck her that *if* Bud was around, and *if* he suddenly sprang out of the fog— "Skip it," she mumbled.

"Pardon?" A bodyless voice croaked beside her.

Now she did run, and reached the Hall panting.

Inside, she blinked in the glare of lights. The cleanup crew was at work, maneuvering trucks expertly in the aisles. Grooms were feeding their charges, horses pawing for breakfast or rattling pans and buckets. In some tackroom a radio played rock. And as she neared Gull's stall he nickered even before he could have seen her.

She fed him, and he ate calmly enough as long as she was with him. She heard him pace about when she went to the tackroom she shared with the Oregon couple. Their black horse was out, no doubt in the ring, with a mob of others.

She'd finished her cleaning when Lee's voice said, "Good morning." He'd never wasted two whole words before Bitsie softened him! "Looks fit," he went on, his gray eyes on Gull. "I'll school you over a few fences this morning. I aim to stick around all day. No telling who might turn up."

"You think Bud might?"

"I kinda hope he does," said Lee in his mildest voice.

The ring was crowded, but its large size suited Gull. After some minutes of warming up, Sis let him gallop weaving between riders and taking advantage of open spots on the rail. When there weren't any, and she came up fast on slower horses, she'd yell "Rail!" and squeeze by. In the center of the ring, men and boys had set up practice fences, which meant staying well clear of horses taking off or landing. Once she swerved hard to avoid a girl who'd fallen, and then again to avoid the girl's loose horse. She kept an eye on Lee, who was helping raise and lower fences or pick up poles while he waited for Gull's turn to jump.

Over it all, a hum of voices and a film of tanbark rose to the roof way up there. Skylights gave ventilation, but not enough, Sis thought. After a long weekend of electric light indoors and darkness outdoors, she'd look a fright.

When Lee signaled her, she rode to the center for his instructions, and checked her girth. Along with others, she kept circling, waiting her turn to jump. The wait was a double one—for their turn, and for free space. But Gull didn't cooperate. He knew why he was here. He *wanted* to jump. What a change from his old self! In protest at restraint, he pranced and tossed his head. He shook flecks of foam from his bit. The reins grew slippery in the sweat of his neck. Sis sat tight, and when the rider ahead of her shouted "Heads up!" and took off, she lined up to go next.

But Lee spoke at her stirrup. "Move aside. We're not jumping." And to the rider behind her, "Go ahead."

At a safe distance he explained, "Gull's too excited now to do the job right. Let's save his fire till tonight. Just let him stand around till he relaxes, then walk him quietly to his stall."

While Sis followed orders, she pondered Lee's strategy. He was counting on Gull's being calm tonight because he'd been made to calm down in the ring instead of charging his fences. Whether he needed the schooling he'd missed was a gamble they had to take.

She talked it over with Lee later in the cafeteria. Through the clatter around them, faces looked drawn, bluish in the harsh lights. Some of the girls still wore hair curlers under scarves and the guys looked in need of a shower and shave. In general, talk was subdued.

Meanwhile, the Oregon people were keeping watch on Gull at Lee's request, and he'd return the favor. No one was to go into Gull's stall, he'd told them. The only exception would be the person testing for drugs tonight.

Sis suspected Lee was worried, though he said, while eating, "We'll do all right tonight, and that's all we have to do, just all right. Maybe in the money some place, but don't expect to win in this company. And if Gull does even pretty good, he'll improve during the rest of the show."

Or else, Sis thought, we can scratch and lose huge entry fees, or get another rider, or cut my throat.

On their way out, Lee said he had business to see to. She should stay with Gull. Then he'd relieve her, and she could walk to the motel for her clothes. "What you need is some air," he added.

Sis's nod amounted to a lie, because what she needed was a new stomach.

At Gull's stall, the Oregon man was upset. He said, "Some dude slapped Gull, over the door, just fooling, and Gull lunged at him. It happened so fast I couldn't stop them. But I sure told him off."

"Gull bit him? My gosh! But who—"

"No, only tried to. But the guy was furious. He talked about suing. Darn rubbish."

"His name couldn't have been Bud?" Sis asked, and her heart gave a nasty lurch.

"Kramer was the name he gave."

It was Sis's turn to be furious. Her anger at Karl Kramer did a lot for her, she realized later. At the time, she scarcely felt her doubts disperse and her nerves steady. She wasn't aware that her expression changed from gloomy to aggressive. A rush of adrenalin had charged her batteries and provided a high of energy and courage.

When Lee returned, she left, having bathed Gull and trimmed him, cleaned tack, and swept the whole aisle. Her neighbor said, "You can come do my housework any time."

"Horsework, yes. Housework, no," Sis answered.

Still high, she spent half an hour cooling a horse for an injured girl groom. She didn't know the girl, but had seen her limping on a slippered foot. She'd felt sorry for her before, and now felt ashamed that she hadn't offered help sooner.

Outside, no more fog. Sunshine was brilliant, buildings clearcut against the bright blue sky. A breeze played with the flags atop the Hall.

But nothing could improve the motel. Sis knew she had time for a nap after her shower, but she wouldn't push her luck. Being alone in this dismal room might bring back her unease. Besides, she couldn't possibly sleep. It was early to change, so she changed only partly, pulling on clean breeches and boots, then a work shirt and sweater. She picked up her hunt cap, good shirt, and jacket, and slammed the door behind her.

On the avenue, she was overtaken by a car full of kids calling her name. It was some of the Tanbark bunch. Sis climbed in their car, and soon all were hurrying to Gull's stall.

After a few private words with her, Lee took off, and she turned back to Gull. He didn't need her now, but neither did she need a lot of chit-chat. At her suggestion, the kids went off to look at other horses and explore the Hall.

Their departure, however, didn't ensure quiet. On the contrary, by feeding time strangers filled the aisles, wanting to see the horses. First in small groups, then in large ones—finally, in a solid queue they pushed along. Some wore formal dress, most likely planning to dine in the Hall's Skydome restaurant before the show. The scrape of shoes on cement and babble of voices rose, while scents of the well-dressed mingled oddly with stable smells.

Sis saw the Oregon wife seated on a stool in front of the black jumper's stall. She herself stood at Gull's door. No one was going to bother him again. The black's owner called to her with a grin, "So how do you like opening night?"

"Exciting!" Sis called back. She was proud that people stopped longer at Gull's stall than at others. Some asked foolish questions, but all were plainly impressed by the tall dappled gray who stood well back, eyeing them haughtily. As one woman put it, "This horse has what's called 'the look of eagles.'"

"Will he fly tonight?" the woman's escort asked Sis, and she answered, "You bet."

She finished changing along with the Oregon wife in their tackroom, hurrying because Lee hadn't returned. But he was there when Sis came out, and she went off to the ladies' room. On her way, she was jolted by sight of a boy who looked like Bud. His back was to her, and in seconds he disappeared in the crowd. No, she decided, he was taller than Bud—wasn't he? But in any case, he was nowhere near Gull.

At the stall she found Jeff, and agreed to have supper with him later. She spoke vaguely, because all at once the loudspeaker came on, testing. It was time for a last grooming, for saddling, for the first call, for Lee's order, "Jocks up."

Suddenly, it seemed, she was headed with other riders for the ring's back gate where the course was posted. There, Lee too crowded in among horses to study it. She saw his face change before she saw the last fence on the diagram.

He said, "It'll be okay."

"I know," she said faintly.

Not all her rivals agreed. They made sick jokes about calling the ambulance. Yet surely they had less reason than she to fear that fence.

She turned Gull to see the actual course in the ring, and gasped at the spectacle. Just then, the band on its platform broke out with the National Anthem.

While shivers tingled her spine, Sis stared at the sea of smooth red tanbark. Islands of vivid jumps rose from it, and, in the center, a canopied and beflowered stand held the officials. Around, the wall of faces stretched to the roof, all facing the spotlit flag at the far end. The lights were too brilliant, Sis thought, music too loud, the tanbark's smell too sharp—but, oh, the whole was thrilling!

There was the rustle of twelve thousand spectators seating themselves. Introductions followed. The judge, the steward, the ringmaster bowed. Sis felt her rivals waiting with her, but she didn't really see them. She heard Lee's "Know your course?" and nodded absently. Seven fences, and then that last one, the eighth. She was conscious only of Gull and of his attitude, a strange poise. It was as if his anger at Karl Kramer had affected him as her anger had affected her. It, or something, had relieved his tension. Then too he'd have caught her cooler mood.

She understood this so well that she thought of herself and Gull as *we*, not he or I. As one, they watched several jumpers go, Gull's ears pricked, his head, like hers, turning to follow each. He stood like a rock, steady as her hands and the grip of her legs.

When the gate swung open for them, she half smiled at the ripple of applause that greeted her beautiful horse. Then such a deep silence fell that she heard a baby's cry high in the stands.

They circled, trotted, then cantered for the first fence, and she *was* Gull, saying, we're over it, a nothing! Now the post and rails, a joke! Here we change leads, we sail over the single bar, over the picket. Toys, all of them! A hind tick at the rustic, but we'll make up for it. Change leads again. The water jump's coming at us, fake water, who cares about that! Little panel next, jumped it so fast the wind of our passage blew off a lath.

We haven't looked at the last fence, though we know it's there. But now we have to turn and face it, the monster. We remember it from the past—but this time it's larger, wider, uglier. It's a killer that can charge and smash us. So take it big. Here it comes! Wait—not yet—wait—*NOW*! A rush, a lift, and, like that eagle, we fly the big stone wall!

Outside the gate, Sis rode clear of the milling horses who hadn't yet gone in. Then she slid off and hugged Gull's neck, and Lee squeezed her shoulder—*Lee* squeezing! He said, ''I've never seen him jump so well, or so willing.''

His words exploded something in Sis's memory. She too had never seen Gull jump as well or as willingly. Now she recalled the boy like Bud who'd disappeared in the crowd, and she felt sick. How ghastly if Gull were tested and found drugged!

''We'll likely place high,'' Lee went on happily. ''This could be the start of a great career for the pair of you, you know that?''

''But Bud—'' Sis began.

''Forget him. I should've told you, he's in custody.''

Limp with relief, Sis let out a shaky breath.

She heard unmistakable voices of the Tanbark bunch nearing. Now they were mobbing her and Gull, and here was Jeff, too, asking, ''What about supper, our date?''

''I'll have to go in again for an award, Lee thinks. But I'll be back,'' Sis told him.

''In ten minutes?''

She laughed. ''You said, 'Come back in ten months.' '' But she suspected the schedule had been changed.